COLLECTION

OF

SHORT

STORIES

By

Nora Kocsis

Collection of Short Stories

Copyright 2008

ISBN:

978-0-6152-0080-4

I dedicate this book to my dear friend,

Gloria McCabe.

Without her unwavering encouragement, gentle push-ing and kind editing, this book would still be a sparkle in my Dear Husband's eye.

Table of Contents

The

Liberty

Bell

The Liberty Bell

It was really sort of neat – listening to the park ranger giving an animated and very interesting history of the Liberty Bell in Philadelphia. As interesting as history can be, at least.

I wanted to get a picture of the Bell. The Ranger's talk seemed to lend an importance to the Bell I had not before considered. I wanted a picture of the side with the crack, and with Independence Hall as background. There must have been a hundred people in the small building, all with the same idea. In gently nudging my way to a more advantageous position, I stumbled over a cane – a white one.

I saw the holder to be an elderly man, with arm outstretched, searching for the Bell. His hand curiously probed the air with firm intent to locate its target. His face was expectant and his sightless eyes stared vacantly in the direction of the Bell.

The old fingers moved slowly forward until their tips touched the Bell. The touch became instantly a caress. The caress held a visible reverence for the century of events the Bell had helped to form.

The old man's eyes came alive, the old face smiled; his entire body reacted to the history the man felt through the touch of the Bell.

His hand roamed over the Bell, tracing the lower edge, left nicked and jagged by unthinking souvenir hunters of days past. His palm felt the cool rough-hewn body of the Bell, stretching up for the inscripted words surrounding the crown.

The gentleman kept his fingers at the letters momentarily, seeming to silently recite the verse there stated. It seemed as though the old man could live all the Bell had seen through his touch.

Again his fingers traced a track on the bell, locating at last the large and historic crack. One lone and bent finger drew down the length of the scar until contact with the bolt was made. The old man's had summarily dismissed the bolt – it was not, after all, part of The Bell.

The aged hand followed the crack to the bottom of the Bell, danced lightly up the body again to caress the letters. The man than gave the Bell a nearly imperceptible pat, as if to say, "Goodbye."

Or to say, "Thank you." Thank you for sharing your soul with me and letting me see the history of my country in you.

As he turned to leave the Bell, his old eyes were still sightless, but no longer vacant. They were filled with the absolute wonder of what he had seen.

End

Cooper Creek

Cooper Creek

There is a very small creek that runs by a town perched on a hillside in Pennsylvania. The creek is called Cooper Creek; it is unknown if that name follows a founding father. The town is more a gathering of folks to be nearby one another than anything else; it is called Conshohocken.

A goodly amount of young children have found their way to the craggy shores of Cooper Creek, and gone home with wet shoes and leggings over the years to be hollered at lovingly by their mothers. But one young child felt very differently about the creek and spent every waking moment he could there. He visioned the creek to be the bounding mane on which his Viking Ship floated toward distant lands and treasures. He hosted pirates and beautiful ladies-in-distress on his ships of many sails and pirate flags.

He even fished in only inches of water with his shoes off and pants legs rolled up, chewing on grass (though he couldn't understand why Huck Finn enjoyed it) and saw imaginary paddle wheel river boats on his Mighty Mississippi.

One time he caught a frog, and thereafter watched every spring for the pollywogs, counting the days as the tails disappeared and little legs sprouted. Then they would hop away to freedom.

The boy tried swimming in Cooper Creek when the spring swelled the creek to a depth in which he could float. But he never thought the snow that melted into his creek would stay so near to the same feel as when it was snow! He jumped out of the creek more quickly than he had jumped in, and shivered a full hour!

The young boy felt like the creek was his – belonged only to him. His dreams were floating on the creek like leaves from the trees. He lived his future life a hundred ways on this body of water, testing each life to see how it felt.

As the boy grew, his dreams grew, but never ventured far from Cooper Creek. He visioned more modern ships, carrying more modern payloads than teas and spices. He looked beyond the shores of Cooper Creek, too, and saw winding roads that nestled off into the trees toward the country afar. He saw the small stores of his town close down and big cars bring noise and bad smells.

It seemed the only thing not changing was his Cooper Creek, so he clung even closer to it. All the warm and comfortable things he had had as a very young boy were still there, floating in the creek like the leaves from the trees. If he looked down the winding roads, they soon became super highways with large dirty trucks and big loud machines whizzing back and forth at enormous speeds.

One day the young man sat under his favorite tree at the shore of Cooper Creek, his eyes followed the creek up toward the mountains which gave it birth. His eyes continued upward toward the vast open sky, and soon rested upon and large and ominous bridge of concrete directly overhead. He had never noticed it before; he was always making his dreams with the creek. It was a super highway. It shadowed Cooper Creek.

The man stood, looked up at the bridge with new eyes, and heard the unmistakable belch of trucks and machines moving at enormous speeds.

He then looked down at his beloved Cooper Creek, and heard the sound of gently running water.

He turned with big steps and, without a backward glance, walked away.

End.

The
Ice Cream
Place

<u>The Ice Cream Place</u>

There is an ever so small window in which to enjoy the ice cream without the company of mosquitoes. The natives of the area know this, and flock to the ice cream shop at the appointed time like high school students at the final bell. A long line forms, its members wiggling and writhing in anticipation of the sweet treat gaining the head of the line permits.

Slowly, the anxious people have their cold prizes in hands and migrate to the few pink tables protected from the bright dusk by pinker plastic umbrellas. They are a happy group, as well they should be with big waffle cones of chocolate-vanilla swirl ice cream, topped with sprinkles and nuts, melting quickly in their hands.

Scanning the seating area brings a myriad of life to the shop. The table on the far left seats a young family of four; Mom trying to keep Baby's chubby fingers out of Big Sister's cup. Big Sister sees the danger to her spoils and quickly pulls the cup away from Baby. The contents fly out of this tightly held container and hit Daddy square in the chest. He grunts, pulls the cold and slimy mess from his T-shirt and redeposits the glob into Big Sister's cup which is now firmly planted on the table. Big Sister sniffs back a tear, grabs her spoon and digs in with abandon. Mom has shifted Baby to the other hip and all the ice cream is now safe.

Close by, a little old lady with wavy blue hair smiles at the scene playing out next to her. She smiles at the young mother and recalls with fondness sitting at the same table with her own young brood so many years before. Her youngest is just now at the window receiving his order of two small waffle cones of strawberry swirl. He has come into town to tell her that he will be bringing a girl home for her to meet. The little old lady is pleased; her youngest son was presenting her with no grand-children and it was high time. With a good job at the computer company she must be smart, and probably had a good bit of money, too. The son sat beside the little old lady and they be-gan to converse about their days and their lives. It was soon apparent that the son was indeed very much in love with this girl. What more could a mother want for her favorite son than to see him happy with a good future in front of him. No matter that the girl was of a different color. That is not as important now as it was in her day. The little old lady sighed, and hoped a silent hope her son would find many happy years and grow old to have ice cream with his own baby one day.

Glancing over her shoulder at the simply gorgeous blue eyes staring at her, the 15 year old girl gave a flirty bat with her eye-lashes. She turned back to the two friends with whom she shared her table and giggled as only a teen girl in love can. The other two girls hid their own giggles under their hands as they tried in vain to concentrate on their fruit smoothies. The young girl couldn't hide her interest in the next table, and had brought her friends out on this Friday night to cover her teen-age stalking of her newest interest. He was just soooooooo gorgeous! His blue eyes just sparkled and his dark hair was always falling in front of them. This was just soooooooooooo sexy! He wore the latest fashions, all the right jewelry, a little ring in his left earlobe but no body piercings she could see, and no tattoos. Her parents would never let her go out if he had a tattoo! The two girl friends were ogling the two boy friends sitting with the Object of Desire, and this fact was not going unnoticed. Soon, the six young people were smiling, chatting, sharing the ice cream and eventually one table. Happy laughter lilted through the air and made for a joyful noise. Their ice cream treats melted slowly in the summer heat as they were forgotten between the giggles and flirtatious peeks from under lashes and sideways James Dean smiles.

The table left by the boys was soon adopted by an old couple. They were quietly spooning their treats into their toothless mouths as they reflected their long lives. He would start a comment and she would finish it. Many years together melded thought processes. Though they had spent many evenings like this – quietly enjoying each other's company – they never tired of the comfortable feeling it brought. Their very first date so long ago had been over a shared ice cream because they could afford only one. Now they were at the end of their lives, at least their lives together. She had been recently diagnosed with a cancer in her brain, and the decision they made together precluded radiation and chemotherapy. After many hours of discussion and research, prayer and contemplation, they decided to go together quietly into this dark night. They had stopped by the bookstore and purchased the latest book published by the Hemlock Society, an organization committed to death with dignity. Many ways to end one's own life were outlined, and the old couple were planning to choose a way to go together before the disease ravaged her brain beyond comprehension. With the book in a brown paper bag on the table, the old man's thoughts were deep and slightly fretful. He reached out and touched her hand which lay limp by her side. She looked at him with eyes that had done the same for more than half a century. Neither spoke, but both understood what they would do. She looked at the clasped hands by her side and a small tear slipped down her old and wrinkled cheek, only to evaporate in the summer heat. He looked into her face and saw only the girl of 19 with whom he had first shared the ice cream so many decades ago. He gave her flaccid hand a squeeze, and they sipped their ice cream sundaes in companionable silence.

A lone young man sat in solitary silence at the table next to the old couple. He had noticed the old man fondly reaching for the hand of his long time love, and the younger one held the hope in his heart that he could enjoy the same thing someday. He had seen, too, the play of the fat baby with the big sister and wished that for himself as well, a family someday. In regarding the flirty and happy banter of the teens, he thought he was not so far away from that himself. He smiled as he contemplated his triple swirl, double dipped cone with nuts. He took a big lick before the melted confection leaked over his hand and down his muscular arm. He knew he had something very important and life changing to do tomorrow, but for this quiet summer evening, he had only to protect himself from the aggressively melting ice cream. The papers in his back pocket were signed and sealed, and meant a going forward for the young man. He had just come from the Army recruiting office, where he had enlisted for 3 years. He had stipulated he be sent to the Middle East, where he felt the biggest threat to his daily life existed. He knew in his heart that ice cream stands like this one would disappear if the awful factions in that part of the world were allowed to expand. He felt it his own patriotic duty to give what he could to insure the fat little baby could grow up to smack Big Sister around. He knew he could contribute much to the daily freedoms of the giggling teens and the little old blue-haired lady. He wiped a wayward stream of melted ice cream with a heavy napkin and reached for the papers. He held them with a reverence he had not realized was within him. He looked at his signature and realized with the stroke of the pen, he had become a man and maybe a hero. He smiled and took a very satisfied lick of the cone. Now how to go home and tell Mom.

The light of the sun was waning, and the moon was waxing full, replacing the warm yellows and reds of the sunset with the soft purple and blue of the night sky. The young family was wiping sticky fingers with damp napkins, Daddy scowling at the large wet and gooey spot in the center of his chest. To the car they were headed, then home for some quiet time after the children were bedded. The son's wallet was opened on the table and pictures presented to the little old lady with blue hair. She was smiling at them, dreaming of pretty little brown babies with curly hair and huge smiles. With a hand at her elbow, the elderly gentleman was guiding his love to their vehicle, at peace with their decision to be together forever, and the teens' laughter filled the air as they pedaled away on their bicycles. The new soldier gathered in all the panorama playing out before him and filed it away in his mind, knowing he would pull these images to review many times as he fought for the very freedoms that made them possible.

It is a good night. And everyone had avoided the mosquitoes.

End

Soft Shelled Crabs

Soft Shelled Crabs

Jane was looking for some soft shelled crabs. Periodically she got a real craving for them. Now bear in mind that her youngest child will be 40 next year, so these cravings are not pregnancy induced. She had kept a trim figure by eating sea foods all her 60 plus years. And though the skin was wrinkled and the short curly hair beginning to grey, she was a vibrant and energetic woman.

She grew up in Florida, and in the 1950's and 1960's, seafood was very plentiful, and free for the catching. Blowfish, trout and catfish were common fare for dinner. Jane's family would even cook and eat the bait her father didn't use. Well, it was shrimp after all.

So growing up on seafood as a staple, it follows that she would want to return to her culinary roots from time to time. That is why she was looking for soft shelled crabs.

Jane looked in the telephone book, but being so far inland, no fish mongers were listed in the yellow pages. She then tried looking on the Internet, and could only find frozen and prepackaged ones. Nuts!

"Maybe the local Publix could special order some," she thought, and jumped in the car to find out.

"May I help you?" came the normal question from the seafood clerk when Jane approached the display case.

"Yes," Jane responded, "I'm looking for some soft shelled crabs. Do you carry them?"

"Only during the spring molting season when they are the most plentiful."

"Can you special order them? I would be willing to pre-pay the order."

"Let me check," the clerk muttered and disappeared through the swinging double doors in the back of the shop.

As Jane waited, she looked over the selection of fish and seafood displayed on ice in the case. There was pink salmon, cut in steaks, dark red tuna, swordfish, catfish – both nuggets and filets. Shrimp curling around themselves and mussels tucked fat end into the shaved ice rounded out the selection. Most of these seafood samples were under signs stating, "Previously Frozen." Only the mussels and bags of small grey clams were missing the sign.

"Yes, I can put in a special order, but the minimum is a gross of crabs". the clerk then named an amount which seemed astronomical to Jane. "The price would be around $600 to $625 when you add in taxes and delivery charges".

Jane balked, "That is really a lot more than I thought! I will have to think about that."

"OK," said the woman. "You just let me know if you want me to place the order. My name is Lucy and I'm in charge of the seafood section. I'm usually here weekdays."

"Thanks. Bye bye." And Jane left the store, more than a little disappointed. She sat in her car for a moment, pondering the possible purchase of a gross of crabs. That much would certainly satisfy her craving. But, oh, $600 plus was prohibitive.

She drove home, disgruntled, silently promising herself to find another avenue to the soft shelled crabs.

A few days later, the ringing of her telephone startled her out of a warm afternoon doze.

"Hey, Cuz. It's Fritz." Came a deep and billowing male voice.

"Hi, Fritz. It's good to hear from you. We haven't talked in just ages! How are things going with you?"

"I know. I just keep myself busy. I just called to touch base with you and see how you and hubby are doing. You gypsies take any trips lately?"

Jane smiled at the label, "No trips, not long ones, anyway. We spent a weekend up near St. Augustine at the alligator farm to see the cranes nesting. That's a sight. What do you hear from your brother, Joseph? Is he still in Charleston?"

"Yep, he had requested the Coast Guard to give him an extension on his enlistment until his 62nd birthday next year, but it was denied, much to his chagrin. Joe was hoping and praying he could round out his entire working career and apply for Social Security right after his separation. Now, his enlistment will be over next month, then he'll be home for good. Forty-one years in the Coast Guard – that's a long time. But he really wanted to make it to an even 42 years."

"What a shame for him. Will he be coming back here, or will he stay in Charleston?" Jane asked her cousin.

"No, he won't stay in Charleston. He still has his house here, so he'll be coming back to that. As a matter of fact, Janie, that's another reason I'm calling. I want to throw a clam bake when he gets back, and I'd like your help with it. I'm just working so many hours, I can't give the planning the attention it needs. Would you mind?" Fritz always sounded a little timid when he asked for something, at least timid for him.

"I'd love to help! But you're the one with all the contacts; you've got to know everybody in Florida! I wouldn't begin to know where to get fresh clams and stuff," smiled Jane, happy to have been asked. Fritz rarely asked for anything. And planning a party was right up Jane's alley.

"Good." The relief in Fritz's voice was deafening. "I sort of have in mind the stuff I'd like to have, if you could run the list down for me, I'd appreciate it. More or less be my legs." He paused, then said with a laugh, "Or be my gopher,"

Jane laughed along with him, responding, "Just like you to take advantage of a relative! But you know I'll do all I can. Can you email me the list and where to get the stuff?"

Fritz grunted, "You know I don't do email; I can barely get that fool computer started to read the news! I'll drop the info off next time I'm in your area."

"That'll work. If I'm not home, leave in on the front porch under the lamp."

"I'll do that, but I'm sure you'll be home."

"How do you know that?"

The doorbell rang just at that moment and Jane asked Fritz to hold on so she could see who was there.

They both gave a hearty laugh when Jane saw it was Fritz.

"Let me go hang up my phone. I can't believe you pulled this off on me. But I'm glad to see you." Jane placed the receiver back into the socket, and turned around to give Fritz a big bear hug. "My God!! Look at you since you gave up the wild life! You look wonderful!!"

A bashful blush danced across the furry face and he said, "I've been working out."

"Well, I guess! And you cut your hair so short! And you grew a goatee!" Jane gushed. The last time she had seen Fritz he had been at nearly 300 pounds. Although he was nearly 6'4", he had been chunky. Now he was trimmed down and looked like a football quarterback at the end of the season. His shoulders were broad and his waist slim. Jane usually saw him in a ratty old T-shirt and shorts. Today he was sporting a snazzy Hawaiian shirt over a snug pair of jeans. He was nearly breath-taking.

"Did you bring me your list?"

Fritz shook his big fuzzy head and said, "No. I thought we could work on that together. Since my wife left, I don't have the benefit of the 'woman's touch,' so I'm depending on you for that."

"Like I said, Cousin, you sure know how to take advantage of your relatives," Jane was laughing as she pulled a chair out from her dining room table. With a wave of her arm, she signaled Fritz to sit in it as she sat across from him. "Let's get started."

They worked on the list of clambake items for nearly two hours, deciding on which sea foods would be grilled, which would be steamed, what would be boiled, and of course some oysters and clams on the half shell.

By the time Fritz left, Jane possessed a detailed and complete clambake menu, and a full list of names and phone numbers of suppliers of such stuff. Fritz had been born and bred on the west coast of central Florida and was deeply ensconced in the proverbial 'Good Old Boy' network. He knew where to get the best and freshest of any kinds of sea foods. He knew sources that the major chain supermarkets didn't dream existed. Fritz knew contacts that bordered on black market. Imagine that, black market oysters and scallops. Jane giggled at that thought. She put the list down, planning to start on it the next day, and returned to the soft and inviting chair to finish her afternoon snooze from which she had been so nicely interrupted.

"Hello, is this Bud?" Jane asked the first name on the list. "My name is Jane and I'm in the market for some fresh seafood, like crabs, shrimp and oysters. Fritz gave me your name. We're planning a clambake for his brother next month. Can you help?"

"Not with oysters, don't do oysters," The voice was gravelly and sounded like it came from a leathery face with a toothless mouth. The verbal cadence sported a strong Florida Cracker accent. "Suckers cut your fingers and hurt like hell. I do shrimp and scallops. Sometimes I git some clams. They got smooth shells, don't bother your fingers none. I stays away from crabs, too. Those suckers clamp onto yer fingers and can nip the end right off. Knew a guy named Nipp who lost most of his baby finger to a crab. Never did do crabs after I saw that. Never forgot his last name, either. He he."

Jane smiled into the phone as Bud rambled, and then said, "Well, we're in the market for shrimp and clams, and maybe some sea scallops if the price is right."

"When do you want 'em? These things don't grow on trees, Little Lady, takes some time to gather enough. Takes goin' to different places to hunt 'em down, too. Crabs kin be persnickety, and shrimp – well, I gots to hunt them at night. Shine a bright light on the water, and when I sees hunerts of little eyes staring back at me, I lets me net go. Get 'em ever time."

"Well, Bud, we need them on the 24th of next month. Does that give you the time you need?" Jane was hopeful. She liked this gruff and sanguine voice immediately and hoped they could do business.

"Twenty-forth, ya say?" Bud paused, rustling some paper. Jane thought he might be looking at a calendar. "That's on a Saturday. Saturday's are always busiest. Saturdays always busy. I don't like Saturdays. Can't do it on Sunday, though. Take the family to church on Sunday. Then big family dinner in the afternoon. Then we play penny-ante with the kids and grandkids. No, Sunday's no good. OK, I'll put you down for Saturday the 24th."

"Thanks, we appreciate that," and gave him the amounts she and Fritz had decided on for the shrimp and crabs.

"OK, got it. It'll be ready on the 23rd if you want to pick it up, or on the 24th if you want it delivered. Extra for delivered, ya know. Gas too expensive to do it for free. Used to. Used to deliver all my stuff for free. Can't no more. Pity. Now who'd you say this is for?"

"For Fritz?"

"Fritz. Fritz? Oh, <u>Fritz</u>!!" Bud clearly had forgotten or had not heard what Jane said at the beginning of the conversation. "I love that Fritz. Like a second son. Been knowin' him since he was in diapers. Pretty momma, he had, and funny dad. Shame the dad died so young and left that pretty momma with all them kids. Took Fritz and his brother out on my boat lots of times when they was young'ns. Taught Fritz how to fish with a little short pole I made just for him. He loved to fish, not like his brother. Brother wouldn't touch a fish or a worm, called them slimy. Sure, I'll make sure to get extra big shrimp and clams for his clambake. Extra big ones. Maybe I can even rustle up some good crabs for him, too."

Jane was relieved and pleased with this special attention at the mention of Fritz's name. The 'Good Old Boy' network certainly had its rewards. "By the way, Bud. Do you ever get any soft shelled crabs?"

"No, not often. Ever onct in a while but not often. Them shells don't stay soft fer long, only a few hours. Don't git a chance to catch many, and if I do, they's usually half eaten up by the other crabs by the time we git 'em out of the traps."

Again, Jane was disappointed, but said pleasantly, "OK, I just thought I would ask. I'll give you a call the week before and firm up arrangements. Here is my phone number if you have any questions. And, Bud, I really enjoyed talking to you."

Jane thanked the gravelly Cracker voice and hung up the phone. She wished she had not asked about the soft shelled crabs. She now felt like she had lost something.

"I have got to stop thinking about those stupid soft shelled crabs!" she admonished herself. "After all, this whole shindig is for Joseph returning home. If he actually does. I should just go make myself a big bowl of fresh oyster stew and be done with it." She let that idea sit in her head for a while, and eventually made her way back to the Publix seafood department for a pint of fresh oysters from Lucy.

The weeks passed quickly as Jane called the other fish mongers on Fritz's list to order the remainder of the clambake tems. She discovered that they all hated to harvest oysters. In their natural habitat, they grew in bunches, much like very large barnacles, and their shells were very jagged and sharp. She finally found a good source from a man with a very long and unpronounceable name which had to contain at least 15 letters. Not only that, but the man spoke with an accent she could barely understand and she wasn't sure he completely understood the order. She did not again ask about the soft shelled crabs. She knew she would receive a negative answer and she just didn't want to feel the discontent again.

Joseph had called Fritz a couple times and on the last conversation told Fritz that he had heard from his commanding officer that his request for extending his enlistment was back on the table, and he was still planning on being back home in a week. But Joseph told Fritz that he didn't plan on unpacking too much as he was still hopeful for a positive outcome on his request.

The list was complete and all the items accounted for. Jane and Fritz had decided to have all the seafood delivered to Fritz's home the morning of the clambake. That way everything would be as fresh as possible, and the fresher seafood was, the better it tasted, and the possibility of contamination was at a minimum. Fritz rented a large number of big galvanized tubs to hold the ice on which to keep the shellfish, and ordered accom-

paniments from the local deli, also to be delivered the morning of the party.

The 24th was approaching quickly. Joseph had returned home,
his official separation date was the end of the month. He would
retire from the Coast Guard with 41 years under his belt. Joseph was glad to be home, but surreptitiously he told Jane that
he would really miss the military life. And was still hoping the
extension until next year would be approved. He was, however, looking forward to the party; he was anxious to see some
of his old friends and family again.

Saturday dawned clear and sunny. Warm by Florida winter
standards and a perfect day for the party. Fritz stayed home to
accept and pay for the deliveries while Jane ran around picking
up paper plates, a 'Happy Retirement' sign and balloons to
decorate Fritz's house. Fritz busied himself setting his BBQ
grills to heat the clams and oysters. He put a huge blue
enamel pot on the stove, the one his grandmother had used to
can the local vegetables Fritz had enjoyed as a youngster. He
filled it with water and his own recipe of seafood seasoning for
the crabs. A multi-layer bamboo steamer was assembled over
a wok full of water – this to steam the mussels and shrimp.
Fritz dug through his kitchen drawers and found 7 oyster
knives. These knives had short fat blades for prying the oyster
and clam shells open. They were not sharp, but very strong to

stand up to the hard prying and twisting to get into the stubborn oysters. Not much else works on oysters; clams usually open as they cook. Mussels were the least precocious, popping wide open as they steam, seemingly proud to offer themselves as delectable seafood treats.

All was ready and assembled. All the seafood laid waiting on the ice and the coals were glowing red waiting to be of service. The crabs were covered with ice, but still scratching the side of the aluminum tub trying to escape. This was going to be fun. And it was all beginning to fill the air with the fragrance of the tropical sea. You could close your eyes and taste the salt air. Ahhh, Florida.

"I can't wait to get started!" Fritz's deep voice had a positive lilt in anticipation of his clambake. "Where in the hell is Joseph? He'd be late to his own funeral. That SOB is going to ruin my party!"

"Fritz, calm down," Jane stated calmly. "It'll be just fine. Look there, he just pulled up."

"Good. 'Bout damned time!"

Joseph walked in, surveying all the fixing and seafood, and whistled softly. "You're really doing it up, aren't you? Then you're not going to like what I have to tell you."

Fritz's head shot up and he looked daggers at his older brother, standing in the kitchen in full uniform. "What the hell?"

"I got a call this morning from my old CO, and he told me to sit tight and be ready to roll. The powers that be had my enlistment extension on their desk right now. I put my home phone on forward to my cell phone. He promised to call as soon as he got the word. If it is approved, I will have to head back to Charleston immediately." Joseph tried not to sound too happy, but had a very difficult time keeping the hope from showing on his face.

"Well, I don't know what to say. What the crap am I supposed to do with all this food?" Fritz whined.

Ever the optimist, Joseph suggested: "My recommendation is to go ahead with the party. You can't really give the stuff back. Plus the fact that a lot of people are planning on being here"

Fritz scowled, "Yeah, to see you! And some from the other side of the state and even farther!" But after a moment of contemplation with his wooly brows furrowed, Fritz's countenance softened and he boasted, "OK then, only the very best for my big brother, whether he's here to enjoy it himself or not!" Fritz said and the men embraced in a big bear hug.

"Hi, Cuz. Good to see you here, too." Joseph turned to hug Jane. "How'r things with you?"

Smiling in the hug Jane said all was fine but was quietly concerned by the news Joseph had brought.

"Well then, let's get this show on the road." And with that, Joseph removed his dress jacket, rolled up his sleeves, grabbed an apron and prepared to dig in.

"Wait! Wait! You can't just go off half cocked and get into this stuff now. I've invited a bunch of people. And they're due here any time." Fritz grabbed his brother's arm and pulled him out of the kitchen.

"But I may have to leave before then. Since it is my party, I should be able to partake early." Fritz's arm was shaken off and the top of the bamboo steamer removed to reveal nice pink shrimp. Joseph grabbed one and peeled it into the sink. He popped the large sea creature in his mouth. "Mmmmmmm, this is so good!" and Joseph grabbed for another one.

Jane and Fritz and Joseph sat around the kitchen table, having light conversation over the threat of a phone call taking Joseph away, slowly and scrumptiously diminishing the inventory of the shellfish.

The friends and relatives began to arrive, and soon the house and yard were filled with laughter and the soft murmur of conversation among old friends. The kitchen was a flurry of boiling water, steaming shrimp, and popping mussels. Outside the oysters baked in their own juicy liquor and the clams opened their shells slightly to admit the pointy oyster knives. Those guests brave enough to try to open a hot oyster right off the grill were rewarded richly with the fresh taste of the nearby Gulf of Mexico.

The dreaded ringing of the phone came like lightening into the hum of the crowd, and the three cousins braced for the news. Good news to one and bad news to the others.

"Yes, this is Joseph." Pause. "Yes, I am requesting an extension of my enlistment." Another pause, this one louder. And longer. "Yes, I understand. Thank you."

Joseph stared at the floor for what seemed like an hour while Jane and Fritz waited.

Fritz couldn't stand it and took his brother's arm and shook it. "What'd they say? What'd they say? Do you have to leave now?"

Joseph slowly looked up at Fritz, and Fritz knew without hearing the words, he could see the deep disappointment in his brother's eyes.

"My request was denied. I'm staying here." Joseph took a shaky breath and once more his eyes embraced the floor for a moment, then moved to caress his beloved uniform hanging militarily on the back of a chair nearby. His two cousins knew it was a personal and quiet moment of mourning.

When Joseph looked up, it was with a crooked smile and he said, "But look at the bright side, now I can eat all the messy oysters and crabs I want. Let me go get some old clothes out of my truck and I'll change out of my uniform." Joseph tried to smile as he said quietly, "For the last time."

Always pragmatic, Fritz said to Jane, "Like I said, let's get this show on the road!" And headed out to man the grills.

Eventually, Fritz left the guarding of the grills to Joseph and took the tub full of crabs into the kitchen. He removed some of the ice, being very careful to keep his pudgy fingers out of harm's way from the claws of the crabs. They were alive, though barely, and still capable of giving a painful nip with their claws. The seasoned water in his grandmother's old blue pot was at a slow boil, perfect for the crabs, and Fritz dropped the big blue creatures into it one at a time.

"Ah, listen to them squeal." Fritz put an ear over the pot. "Music to my ears! Jane, did you know that's air escaping from their lungs when they hit the hot water? The crabs are cold-blooded and don't feel any pain. When I was a kid my father told me that they were screaming 'Save me! Save me!' to get out of the water and for the longest time I wouldn't eat a crab. Silly me."

"Yes, Fritz. I did know that. I grew up here, too, remember? My father told me the same thing!" Jane's smile was iridescent with the happiness of the day.

Fritz had cooked most of the crabs and the tub was nearly empty. When he picked up the last crab, he discovered a plastic bag, sealed against the water, on the bottom of the tub.

"Hmmm, what the hell is this?" Fritz picked up the bag and shook the water and ice off it. Inside there were 5 crabs and a note. He read the note and smiled.

"Hey Jane. Come back to the kitchen." He called out.

"What is it? I was just gaining ground on an oyster."

"You have an admirer." Fritz handed her the wet and dripping bag.

Jane looked at the bag and the five crabs in it. "Why don't you cook these, too?"

"They're for you. There's a note."

"Where? Oh, I see it." She read slowly. She smiled and put her   hand   on   her   chest. "That's just so sweet. I can't believe he did this."

The note was from Bud, the gravelly, toothless voice to whom she had spoken last month. It told her he had found some soft shelled crabs and put them aside just for her.

Jane quickly raided Fritz's cabinet for a shallow pan and the refrigerator for some butter. She took the wok and bamboo steamer off the stove and heated the butter in the pan.

"Look, Fritz! He even cleaned them! Want one?"

"I wouldn't take food out of your mouth! Are you kidding? I know how much you love those things." But after a short pause, "maybe a couple-a legs." Fritz couldn't refuse them completely.

When the butter was just right, Jane dropped the first soft shelled crab into the pan. The sizzle was captivating; the fragrance divine. They were small crabs and all five fit into the large pan. The legs and claws turned brown, then bright red, indicating they were done. Jane removed them from the pan and placed them on paper towels to drain the butter, then on a plate. She broke off a claw and 2 of the legs which Fritz had in his mouth in a flash.

"Mmmmmm. I had forgotten how good these taste. Your mother could do them up right. Soft shelled crabs and fish roe." Fritz stopped cooking for a moment as he savored the taste and conjured a happy childhood memory.

Jane was at the table with the crabs on the china plate in front of her. "You sure you don't want one? Speak now or forever hold your peace!" She offered once more to Fritz.

"No, Hon, you go ahead and enjoy."

Jane pulled one of the legs from the body and slowly closed her mouth around it. "Oh, this is wonderful!" she thought. It tasted of the sea, of ages past, of her childhood, and slightly of good butter.

It took her nearly half an hour to eat the soft shelled crabs. When the last one was gone, she felt happy and sated. The gravelly old voice had remembered what she said, and taken the time and trouble to separate the soft crabs from the others, also keeping them from the water which would have hardened their shells. What a sweetheart. Jane promised herself she would send Bud a nice thank you note as she savored the lingering taste.

Life was good. With friends and family around, laughing, enjoying the good food and camaraderie, she could only thank God for the blessings of those things and of family like Joseph and Fritz.

And soft shelled crabs. Yum!

End.

The

Helping

Hand

The Helping Hand

Her hand pushed cautiously through the unpleasant airport air intent upon gentle contact with the old and bowed shoulder. But Amanda eventually drew back her gloved hand, stepping up to close *** the distance between old lady's woolen coat her own light suede jacket. She took a small tentative step forward, not wanting her height to startle the elderly woman. Amanda tucked her wavy brown hair behind her ear as she bent down and with soft respect asked, "Excuse me, Ma'am. May I help you to the luggage area?" Amanda's voice was barely audible from the emotion she felt. Her heart beat so that she could feel it in her fingers as the old blue eyes smiled up into eyes the same hue and gladly accepted the younger woman's offer.

Amanda was returning from a business trip, exhausted and rumpled after the overnight flight which had landed in Atlanta's Hartsfield Airport just after 6:00 AM. Amanda's lanky frame normally held clothing well, but after five hours in an airline seat, her tweed skirt was wrinkled at the knees and waist, and her highly polished short boots had lost their luster. The little woman to whom she was speaking had been on the same aircraft and Amanda had noticed her walking the aisle to the rear of the plane, looking elegant as only a very old woman can.

At first, the short and curly white hair caught her eye, but Amanda ignored the sensation because it had happened so many times before. "All little old ladies look alike," Amanda admonished herself. However, each time Amanda caught a different look at the elderly woman, there were more and more similarities to her own late mother. Amanda's mother had a straight and rather long nose for her small face; this little woman had the same feature. Mother had finely arched brows that framed the vivid blue eyes which carried mirth at their edges. When the diminutive lady smiled, however gently, the same lines of life appeared. In the small woman's lap was a piece of finely crocheted lace, and the fingers working on it were bent and gnarled as they commanded the small hook to make its fine knots.

Amanda got very little rest on the flight from San Diego, staring surreptitiously at the tiny frame taking up so little space in the airline seat. There were so very many similarities that Amanda was convinced the woman could have been her mother.

Amanda's mother had died suddenly just 3 years before, in her father's arms of a massive stroke. Her body had been immediately cremated, and her ashes strewn on a small lake in her hometown in Pennsylvania; there had been neither a funeral nor memorial service. Amanda had felt cheated at that, consequently never really accepting that her mother was gone. And here, so many months later, sat a person indistinguishable from the real thing. Amanda was slightly shaken. The details of this little being were more than striking, right down to the dark age spot just below her left eye and the small triangular gap between her front teeth.

Amanda had deplaned first, but did not hurry to leave the gate area, opting to poke around at the magazines across the concourse to get a better look at this old woman. Amanda was not disappointed. The lady was last to come off the airplane as she was being helped into a wheelchair by one of the flight attendants. She had donned a pair of short white gloves and a small close-fitting hat that matched her worn wool coat. The elderly eyes smiled up at the young man and her bent and twisted fingers handed him a bill as she thanked him for his help. The busy attendant thanked her, pocketed the bill and scurried off to get another plane loaded and off the ground.

That left the little woman alone in the wheelchair, and she appeared more than a little confused. This is when Amanda approached her with the offer for help and was accepted.

"Have you been to Atlanta before?" Amanda asked in a more normal voice than she felt.

"No, and my son is to meet me, but I see he is late again. I would greatly appreciate any help you have time to offer." And as she reached into her purse added, "I can pay you for your time."

Amanda promptly refused payment of any sort, and rounded the wheelchair to grasp the handles and began to push the small woman toward the luggage carousel.

Amanda gave the chair a gentle nudge, not wanting to give the woman a bumpy ride, and the wheels did not move. Though the 'nudge' had been assertive, the chair resisted, Amanda nearly tripped and landed in the chair with the lady. Amanda was embarrassed and apologetic, but the old woman's face immediately erupted with laugh lines and straight teeth in a smile. It was a friendly smile and both women saw the humor in the incident.

"Maybe it would work better if you released the brakes on the wheels." The smiling face suggested. "By the way, my name is Kathrine, Kathrine Bigelow." And she held out a hand in friendship.

The gesture helped Amanda over her discomfort and the two women shook hands, soft manicured fingers touching soft kid-gloved hands. Amanda reached down and pulled the levers back, releasing the tension on the hard rubber wheels. This time, when Amanda nudged, the chair went smoothly forward.

"My name is Amanda. I live here in Atlanta. If your son doesn't come by the time we retrieve your luggage, maybe I can help you get somewhere?"

"Oh, no, but thank you. He'll be here. He generally runs late but I've only been stranded a few times over the years. I'll be fine."

This statement made the hair on Amanda's neck stand straight out. Even after such a short acquaintance, it was obvious this was an intelligent and gracious lady. "Well, we'll probably find him at the luggage carousel. With security being what it is at the airports now, relatives rarely can meet the planes at the gates. I'll stay with you until he comes."

Kathrine smiled Amanda's mother's smile and responded, "A young and pretty thing like you probably has many suitors waiting for your return. I'll be just fine. But I appreciate the offer. And the company will be nice."

The wait for the elevator was long, and the interval between trains to the main terminal was lengthy and quiet this early in the day. Hartsfield didn't really wake up to full schedule for a good hour or so. But the ride from E Gates, though the farthest to the main terminal, was smooth and comfortable. The women took the time to chat a bit.

"Have you lived in Atlanta all your life?" Kathrine queried.

"No, I was born in New York, raised in Florida, and live here now working for WSB Channel 2, as a newscaster."

"What interesting work that must be! To know all the facts and information of the day before anyone else." She let her mind savor the thought and the privilege. "You are so fortunate! How did you happen here?"

Amanda looked skyward in recall and told Kathrine, "I guess it started in high school. My brother found out that if you worked on the school paper, you could get into all the sporting events for free. With that in mind, I made sure one of my classes was journalism so I could work on the paper. My brother did it to avoid paying for his tickets; but I soon discovered there weren't many girls allowed to talk to the football players on the field and I just loved it. I ended up married to one."

"In my high school, I was one of four in the graduating class. My older sister was the teacher so I had to mind my P's and

Q's." Kathrine smiled up over her shoulder at Amanda.

"Please tell me more about that. I have often heard of one-room schoolhouses, but honestly wondered if they actually existed." Amanda's journalistic training and curiosity had kicked in so her mind was receptive to any new information. Besides, she was beginning a genuine affection to this tiny woman, and threads of a protective instinct were beginning to weave around her heart.

Kathrine gave a musical laugh – reminiscent of years gone by – and began her description of life in a small Pennsylvania town. The town sat on the crest of a hill in north-eastern Pennsylvania, and was very small. The entire complement of students totaled 12 when no one was ill or home helping with a harvest. "I remember the old wood stove in the front of the schoolhouse. We would be freezing in the winter until one of the farmers brought in some of the wood from a tree he had cleared from his farm. We would push five or six logs into the stove, and within an hour we had the door and all the windows open to cool the place out." Kathrine's chuckle made Amanda enjoy the mental image which reminded her of the kerosene heater in her own kitchen as a child.

"Was your family large?" Amanda was interested as she had only one sibling.

"By today's standards, yes, we had a large family. There were 7 of us children, but one died at birth, so 6 were left to do all the work." The last comment was the first negative appearance on Kathrine's face that Amanda had seen. Amanda had read historical accounts of those times and of families becoming too large to care properly for all the children. Parents were forced into the choices of giving the children up to churches or other families who were childless, or chance the death of family members. She knew it was a difficult time in the history of the country, especially in the rural areas where families depended upon themselves so completely.

"What work was that? Did you have a farm to run?" Amanda was truly interested, but didn't want to seem pushy or as though she were interrogating.

"My father was responsible for the breeding or raising of some sort of animals. But he did not work around the house, so I have assumed he was a hired hand on someone else's place. He developed dementia very early and I never heard many details. Frankly, I didn't really care to know. I loved to read, so I didn't pay much attention to much else other than my books. Even now..." Kathrine opened her satchel and revealed 4 thick paper-back books. "I still love to read, but now I don't have to climb up into a tree to hide from chores to do it." Again,

Amanda's mother's smile and mischievous twinkle filled her heart.

"You would love my book collection." Amanda offered. "I, too, love to read and my friends all know it. Most holidays I can expect books, sometimes first editions and sometimes even signed by the authors. I am most proud of those. Maybe you'll have a chance to see my collection one day."

The two women chatted companionably until the train slowed and the computer broadcast announced the main terminal was the next stop. Amanda gathered her purse and scarf then checked that Kathrine left nothing behind. Kathrine arranged a hopeful look on her aged face, scanning for her son in the throng of people milling about as Amanda pushed the wheel-chair out of the train and headed toward the baggage claim area.

"Do you see him? Tell me what he looks like and I'll help you look. Sometimes my height is a real advantage." Amanda was referring to Kathrine's son, expected to meet his mother and take her from the airport.

"Well," Kathrine began her description, "He is quite tall, too, and thin, and has been wearing his hair very long but keeps it in a queue at the nape of his neck. It's wavy, his hair, and grey in

front but receding a bit at his forehead and on the top."
Kathrine chortled. "I believe he keeps his hair long to try to hide
his bald spot. He doesn't wear glasses. He seems to have a
lot of gold chains around his neck and I think an earring in one
of his ears." She shook her head and said under her breath,
"That, of course could describe better than half of the people
who make Atlanta their home. Especially if they live in Buckhead. I'm sorry I'm not better help."

"What is his name? If we don't find him, we'll have him paged
to meet us." At this idea from Amanda, Kathrine perked up a
bit. Amanda had the distinct impression that if her son did not
appear, she had no place to go.

"His name is John Gold; at least it is an easy one."

Amanda rolled Kathrine to the luggage carousel and waited for
the luggage from their flight to start coming down the ramp and
onto the circular conveyor belt. It was no wonder things were
broken and bags ripped and ruined with the way they were
handled harshly and thrown indiscriminately at the conveyor.
All the bags looked so similar; Kathrine sat back and wondered
at how the passengers knew which one was their own.
Amanda soon returned with two of her bags and the mystery
was solved. Aside from a large tag with Amanda's name
prominently displayed, she had tied a huge pink nylon bath

sponge to the handle. That made the octogenarian giggle.

"I only have one more to get, tell me which ones are yours and I will pull them all over here, too."

Kathrine pondered her lap and said quietly, "I only have one. It is an old suitcase with hard sides and no wheels. It is beige with two brown stripes going around it which look like straps but really aren't. There are no zippers, it has the old fasteners that you push a button and the lever pops up. I haven't seen too many so it should be easy to spot." She looked around again, "I wonder where John is."

Kathrine was becoming more and more concerned that her son had not yet appeared. Amanda, on the other hand, was getting madder by the minute.

The remaining luggage retrieved, Amanda signaled for a sky-cap with a cart onto which to load the four pieces. Kathrine's suitcase was very small, not much larger than an old-fashioned makeup case. Kathrine saw Amanda looking at her small case and volunteered, "I have some clothes at John's place, so I really do not need to carry much with me." She looked around again with furrowed brow. "He should be here by now."

"Shall we go to the Travelers' Aid station and have him paged?

Maybe he isn't sure of the flight number or airline." Amanda suggested this and hoped Kathrine would be amenable to the idea.

"I never knew you could do that." A voice of wonder came from Kathrine. "I always thought the 'Travelers' Aid' was for foreigners and not for people who live here."

"That is a common misconception," Amanda told her new friend, and asked the skycap with the cart if he could take them there.

Seeing a large tip in his future, he offered, "Follow me, that desk is on the other side of the terminal." And pushed his heavy load much more easily than Amanda pushed her minute load in the wheelchair. Amanda could barely keep up.

Suddenly Kathrine came alive, "There he is! There he is! Its John! He's right over there by the elevator! In the yellow jacket. See him?"

Amanda saw the tall lanky man standing there, but he looked Caribbean or Hispanic. She took Kathrine closer to him and Kathrine's expression told Amanda all she needed to know. It was not John.

Amanda had to nearly run to catch up with the skycap and their luggage, but managed to do so just as he reached the Travelers' Aid desk.

"I wonder if we could have someone paged?" The volunteer seated behind the desk turned a lazy face towards Amanda. "Wadja say, Honey?" She was a heavy woman with a round face, 1960's make-up and yellow bee-hive hair that had probably not moved for 40 years. Amanda guessed her age to be nearly 70, though through her makeup, she was trying to reach back to a more alluring time. Her name tag said '*Bunny,*' so Amanda addressed her as such.

"Yes, Bunny. My friend is looking for her son who was to meet her here and we have not been able to hook up with him. Is it possible for you to page him for us?"

Bunny brought her rotund figure out of her chair to peer over the desk at Kathrine. Kathrine had the wherewithal to look frail, dismal and nearly tearful for the inspection. As Bunny settled back into her groaning chair, she said to Amanda, "Aw, poor old lady. Sure, Sweetie, I'll page him. What's his name?"

"John. John Gold. And thank you." Amanda had learned long ago that contrition to public servants, even volunteers, went a long way. "We really appreciate any help you can give."

About that time, Bunny spotted the skycap standing behind the two women, gave him a snarly smile and a bodacious wink. She apparently had no problem with the 30-plus year age difference between them. The skycap turned around quickly to check the luggage, balancing it carefully and watching it with rapt attention.

Bunny shrugged and picked up the microphone. "Paging John Gold. Mr. John Gold," Bunny breathed into the microphone with a Marilyn Monroe voice. "Please meet your party at the Travelers' Aid Desk in the South Terminal. Paging John Gold. Mr. John Gold. OK, Ladies, there's a couple chairs there by the door; I'm sure he'll be here in a minute."

"We thank you so very much." And knowing the answer should be no, Amanda asked, "Do we owe you anything for your service?"

"Oh, no, Honey. That's part of my job here. This is Travelers' Aid, ya know." Bunny was answering Amanda but trying to get the attention of the Skycap who was diligently fussing with the baggage on his cart. It was becoming obvious that Bunny had a reputation and he wasn't about to be part of it.

The trio found the chairs by the door and Amanda settled into one, Kathrine positioned herself beside them, and the Sky-cap maneuvered the large cart toward the wall.

"Ma'am?" He sought Amanda's attention. "Would you like for me to unload these bags here for you?"

She thought for a moment, considered that John might not show up at all, and decided it was better to keep him around. "No, thank you. We may need you to take them to my car in the North Terminal parking area."

Seeing an even larger tip, the Skycap tipped his hat with a respectful, "Yes, Ma'am. Whatever you like." He then took one of the chairs and moved it behind the cases piled high on the cart, well out of Bunny's line of vision and took a seat.

Hours went by, or at least seemed to. Actually, it was only about 20 minutes. Kathrine appeared to become more agitated as the time lumbered by. At the half-hour mark, Amanda could stand it no longer and went back to speak to the daunting Bunny.

"I'm so sorry to bother you again, but could I ask you to repeat your page? It would mean a great deal to his mother." Amanda put on her best trite and submissive air and Bunny responded immediately.

"That was John Gold, right?"

"Yes," and knowing that unearned compliments carried a lot of weight, Amanda said, "you have a good memory."

"Sure, Honey." And Bunny brought her breathless voice to the microphone and repeated the page.

"Thanks again." And Amanda walked back to sit in the cracked and rickety chair.

"Do you think he heard this one?" Kathrine was very concerned. To Amanda the level of emotion seemed out of symmetry with the situation, so she tried to introduce some humor by saying, "Any man that doesn't respond to a voice like that over a loud speaker must have lost his hearing!" And that did bring a less serious face to Kathrine. It brought an audible chuckle from the Skycap hiding behind the luggage.

Kathrine, Amanda and the Skycap waited until the sun was high overhead. Kathrine's curly white head bobbed as she dozed, nearly losing her small hat. Amanda decided enough was enough and asked the Skycap to stay by Kathrine to insure her safety and marched over to the Travelers' Aid desk again. Bunny had been replaced by a very staunch and unfriendly looking woman, but her demeanor belied her appearance; when she smiled her face lit up and invited questions from the weary and confused travelers. The name tag on her blue blazer stated Eunice, and she seemed to personify the image of such a moniker. Amanda explained the situation, so Eunice asked if she should repeat the page.

"No," Amanda contritely answered, "It has been nearly 2 hours and as you know we have paged several times. Its evident to me that this poor woman's son is not available. But if I could leave her son's name and my name and contact number, it might be a help. Her son's name is John Gold, his mother's name is Kathrine Gold and mine is Amanda Bigelow. She stated her phone number and Eunice repeated it to make sure she had it written correctly." Amanda was more comfortable with not having to pussy-foot around this woman who seemed assured of herself and her job. She told Eunice, "I do so appreciate your efforts. Let's just hope we get a response."

"Yes, I hope so, too. I will keep this note in a prominent place so the next shifts will see it as well. I hope everything turns out well for you. And say hello to Bill for me."

"Bill?" Amanda was puzzled.

"Why yes, your Skycap. One of the nicest young men I've ever met."

Amanda walked back over to the chairs which had become home for so long, and first delivered the message from Eunice. Bill immediately popped up from behind the luggage with a huge smile and an animated wave. It was returned in kind.

"Kathrine?" Since she had been dozing, Amanda touched her softly and called her name quietly. "Kathrine, we're going to go now."

"But what about John? He hasn't come yet." Kathrine was clearly agitated and mentally thrusting about for some sensible conclusion to her dilemma.

"I left your name and my phone number with the new lady at the Travelers' Aid desk. She has it posted where all the shifts can see it. They will page periodically until the airport closes tonight. He will be sure to hear the page no matter when he arrives, and get my number to call you. You have his number, don't you?" Amanda admonished herself that she hadn't thought of this before now.

"I have an old one. He just moved from Roswell to Buckhead and was going to give me the information when I came into town." Nothing Kathrine could offer seemed that John even wanted to help his mother. It was difficult for Amanda to remain calm; she had adored her own mother so and would have never treated her this way. Kathrine was so upset she was nearly in tears. Without her son, she was stuck in a strange city with no place to go.

"Do you want me to take you to a hotel? There are some fine ones nearby."

Kathrine's misty eyes looked up to Amanda and asked the price of a room. When Amanda told her she could probably get a nice safe room for about $150.00, Kathrine's face melted and her whole body seemed to shrink down into the wheelchair.

Amanda thought quickly and told her, "Well, I'll tell you what. It's only about 1:00 in the afternoon, and you can't check into any of the hotels before 4:00 or 5:00, so why don't we go get a bite to eat and we'll have better ideas on a full stomach." Kathrine still wasn't convinced, so Amanda quickly added, "A good friend of mine owns a diner on Peachtree Street and owes me a couple meals. Why don't we go collect? Are you as hungry as I am?"

As she was talking, Amanda had already unhooked the brakes on the wheelchair, motioned Bill the Skycap to follow along, and gave a final wave and smile to Eunice behind the desk.

Before Kathrine could object or agree, she was on her way to Amanda's car in the nearby North Terminal parking lot.

They found the car easily, a shiny green SUV, not too big, but still too tall for Kathrine to enter gracefully. Bill lifted Kathrine into the leather passenger seat and helped with her safety belt. The small woman was nearly lost in the large puffy seat. Kathryn thanked him and handed him a bill. He refused it politely, held her skirt out of the way of the door and closed it quietly beside her.

This simple action was not lost on Amanda, but was indicative of Bill's general personality. As they sat in the chairs, Bill hiding from Bunny, Amanda had discovered he was a college student and this part-time job helped him with extra spending money. She reached into her purse and folded two $50.00 bills to reward him for his help and company for the past few hours.

Bill accepted the tip, glanced at the $50 and told Amanda "This is mighty generous, Ma'am. Thank you." About that time he realized there was another one and gazed at Amanda, big black eyes wide and mouth open, speechless.

"You earned every cent. Please accept this with my thanks for being so patient with us and helping more than you realize." She touched his arm lightly.

Bill croaked a weak but heartfelt "Thank you so much!" and rolled the luggage cart and wheelchair back toward the outside baggage check in area.

Amanda jumped into the drivers' seat, happy to have the familiar feeling of worn and fitted seat, put the key into the ignition and the engine purred to life. She pulled the parking ticket from behind her sun visor, checked the date on it, and reached for her wallet in preparation to pay her way out of the long-term parking lot.

Kathrine, who had sat quietly through the last few minutes of activity outside the car, held Amanda's hand away from her purse and tried to push some bills into her hand. Amanda could not quickly think of a good reason to refuse, so reluctantly accepted. However, when they got to the pay station, the amount was far more than Kathrine had given, so Amanda just pretended most of it was change and returned it to her with a smile.

"Got off easy on that one, didn't we?" Amanda's easy demeanor made giving the cash back a very natural thing to do. Amanda did not know how much money Kathrine had, but judging from the reaction when Amanda quoted the price of a moderately priced hotel room, probably not too much.

They left the airport and headed north on I-285, and just before they turned onto Route 400, Amanda pointed to a modern building with a round glass front and told Kathrine that was where she worked.

"That's a beautiful building! It looks new." Kathrine observed.

"It is fairly new. This one took the place of an old brick building that had been built in the '40's. The same company was still in business about 10 years ago, so WSB decided since they had done such a good job on the first one, let them do the second one. And we never missed a broadcast, on TV or either radio station. It was quite a thing to watch! And this new building is just amazing. It is the very first television station capable of broadcasting in true high definition!" Amanda couldn't help but brag about her job or the building in which she did it.

In only minutes, Kathrine was fast asleep, her head supported by the seat belt. Amanda smiled, decided to skip the Peachtree restaurant, and turned onto Route 400. The normally jammed highway out of Atlanta was wonderfully traffic-free, and the ride to Amanda's exit was smooth and pleasant. Once reaching Marietta, Amanda turned off the highway and wound around the local roads to her home.

"Kathrine, wake up. We're here." Amanda's voice wedged softly into Katherine's sleep.

"Where?"

"At my house. I thought you might like to freshen up a bit after such a long flight and sitting in that noisy airport. Can you make it up the sidewalk? If not, I have a walker which belonged to my mother. I could get that for you in just a second."

Kathrine thought for a moment through her still groggy mind, then said, "It doesn't look too far. If I could hold your arm, I'm sure I'll be fine."

Amanda gladly helped the diminutive person from the car and supported her with an arm around her tiny waist. Reaching the porch, Amanda unlocked the door and led Kathrine to an easy chair in the front room. "I'll be right back with the luggage, and then we'll get you a place to freshen up." She turned and left before Kathrine could say a word.

Alone in the room, Kathrine took the pleasure of being nosey when no one could catch her. She looked all around the room and felt instantly comfortable. There was a heavily upholstered sofa in front of a large picture window, flanked by occasional oval tables at each side. The tables held large but delicate lamps resting on beautiful old doilies. A chair and ottoman matching the sofa occupied one corner and a floor lamp seemed assigned to that area alone. The chair in which she was seated was a modified wing chair, the fabric complement- ng the other upholstered pieces. A lot of careful thought had gone into the decorating of this room and it was beautiful as well as comfortable.

Just in front of her, Kathrine noticed a small footstool which was covered in needlepoint; so lovely. She reached to run her fin- gers over the fabric. The telltale uneven weft of the fabric indi- cated it was hand worked.

Just then Amanda returned, carrying Kathrine's small case. "Kathrine, I have a guest room right down the hall with a little bath area where you can freshen up. As a matter of fact, my mother used to stay there when she visited since she couldn't navigate the stairs. Her walker is in the closet if you would like to use it while you are here."

"I certainly don't want to take advantage of your kindness or hospitality, but I could surely use some fresh water on my face and a comb in my hair. Thank you."

So the two women went down the hall, the short one turning into the guest room and the tall one proceeding on to the kitchen.   Since Amanda had been away from the house for so long, there was little fresh produce in the fridge. She did find an unopened bag of romaine hearts in good condition and a can of Albacore tuna in the pantry; there were frozen English muffins which were defrosted quickly in the microwave.

Amanda put a kettle of water on the stove and pulled out two pretty teacups and lay a tea bag by each. She cut up a lemon which had been lurking in the produce drawer of the fridge, found a small box of long-life milk in the pantry, and added the sugar bowl to the table. She was just setting out the flatware when Kathrine entered the kitchen, having accepted the use of the walker.

"Oh, my." Kathrine gushed, "You didn't have to do all this on my account! This is just lovely."

"All I did was put one extra of anything I would have done for myself. This is just canned tuna and lettuce on an English muffin and a cup of tea. It isn't a standing rib roast with Yorkshire pudding!"

That did bring a smile to Kathrine's face. Amanda surveyed the face and saw that it seemed less stressed. Kathrine had removed her gloves and coat and little hat as well as combed her hair so it had fewer curls all over her head.   Amanda was pleased that her mother's walker was being used, though it did give her an eerie sensation. At first glance, Kathrine coming through the kitchen door had stopped Amanda's breathing for a moment until she realized this woman was not her mother; her mother had been gone for years.

The tuna sandwiches and tea were devoured quickly, and to Amanda's surprise, Kathrine reached for a second one. She was such a tiny woman – where was she putting all this food! She was on her third cup of tea, as well.

They shared the clearing of the table and after Amanda completed loading them into the dishwasher, she asked Kathrine if she would like to rest in the small room for a while. It had been a grueling flight from the west coast and then the tense hours waiting for her son, John.

"I am so pleased you offered. I was so hoping to do just that but didn't want to impose on your gracious hospitality. If you don't mind, a nap would do me nicely." Kathrine was obviously relieved and very appreciative of the offer, turned to toddle down the hall with the help of the walker and disappeared through the door. Moments later Amanda heard the slow even breaths of a serene and peaceful sleep.

That was the signal for Amanda to get to work. She first

grabbed her phone book and looked up Gold, John. The book revealed two John Golds and six J. Golds. One of the two John Gold listings was in Roswell; what good luck to find it so quickly! She dialed the number and the computer voice told her the number had been changed or disconnected and was no longer in service.

She tried the other John Gold and found it to be a wrong number. Amanda then tried dialing Information, but there was no listing either in Roswell or Buckhead and the operator even took the time to check new listings in the surrounding areas. Stymied, Amanda sipped her cold tea and tried to think. With all the resources she had as a journalist for a large metropolitan area, she should have some means of finding one John Gold. She would nose around tomorrow when she returned to her office.

Meanwhile, she had to find a way for Kathrine to stay here where Amanda knew she was safe.

That opportunity presented itself more quickly and easily than Amanda had ever imagined. When Kathrine awoke, Amanda was sitting in the front room reading a novel by an exciting new author. She was so enthralled with the story that she didn't realize Kathrine had entered the room until she heard the walker squeak. Amanda quickly marked her place and put the book on the needlepoint footstool.

"Well, you look refreshed. How was your nap?" Amanda was pleased to see the change in her new friend.

"It was just what this old body needed. Thank you for asking." Kathrine sat quietly on the sofa in front of the picture window. She paused, seemingly searching for words.

"My dear, dear Amanda, you have been so kind to me, a perfect stranger. You have stood by me and taken valuable time from your busy life. You have invited me into your home and given me a soft pillow on which to rest my head."

Amanda opened her mouth to reply, but was silenced by the wave of an old and twisted hand.

"I know you are going to say I am welcome, I am no bother, you love to help and other things like that. At one point when I was younger and my life was like yours, I would have done much the same thing. That is why what I am about to say is so very difficult for me."

Again, Amanda waited quietly for Kathrine to continue. She carefully kept a soft countenance on her face, sensing intuitively Kathrine was struggling.

"As you know, Amanda, my son John has not come forth as he had promised. I was depending so on his help, but frankly, not expecting it." The old woman's demeanor became frailer with each word she spoke and she was obviously ashamed of her plight. "The apartment building in El Cajon in which I have lived for the past 28 years was recently sold and we residents were given the option of purchasing our apartments for several hundred thousand dollars or vacating in 30 days."

Amanda knew this type of thing was happening all over the country and Southern California seemed to have among the most aggressive developers. She could only guess what would come next from Kathrine and how terribly difficult it would be for her to admit. So she listened quietly and intently, waiting patiently through the pauses Kathrine took to regain her composure.

The soft blue eyes looked into Amanda's and continued in a low voice. "As you have probably surmised, I am not a woman of means. I receive a small Social Security check, and in California I made custom doilies, tablecloths, bedspreads and such for special order through some of the more upscale department stores. The revenue I earned from that made up the deficit so I could remain in my small apartment by my friends. Now all that is gone." Kathrine gazed out the window and murmured, "All of it gone."

Kathrine took a breath and paused again. An unwilling tear worked its way through the maze of lines left by a lifetime of gaiety and descended past her chin to float through the sunlight and land on her folded hand. "I have no resources, no savings, nothing but what I could bring in my small valise." She took a deep and shaky breath and said, "Could you find it in your heart to allow me to stay with you for a few days until I can find my son and my situation improves?"

Amanda could barely contain her own tears as she looked at this woman who found herself so alone and forgotten in a strange place. She could only be thankful of the opportunity to aid this woman and relieve her despair. Amanda walked around the little stool and sat by Kathrine on the sofa. She embraced the little woman and Katherine melted into her strong arms.

"Of course you may stay. I was trying to think of a way to ask you to do just that without offending you. You will be such company to me. I thank you for asking."

It was apparent Kathrine was very relieved; she had seen herself on the street without the help of her only son. "I just don't want to be a burden to anyone. Maybe there is something I can do for you? You have such a lovely home. I noticed you have an antique dining room table. I would love to design and crochet a tablecloth to go on it."

Amanda was delighted. "Only if you allow me to pay a fair market price for it. Oh, that will be so lovely. I have often thought of a lacy cover for it, and for the sideboard. So I can offer you two projects. My mother used to crochet. She liked doing intricate tablecloths and bedspreads. She used the fine cotton that looked to me like she was working with a piece of hair!"

Kathrine's mood brightened considerably as they spoke of tablecloths and things familiar to her. Amanda watched her demeanor change and the faint glimmer of an exciting, intelligent and creative woman was beginning to emerge.

"You know," Amanda said thoughtfully. "I don't know if you noticed, but the closet in your room has some of my mother's clothes. I haven't taken the time to go through them. It would be a great help to me if, in your spare time, you could take a look at them. As a matter of fact, you are about the same size as she, so you are welcomed to any you like. Anything else will only go to the thrift store. I think I prefer someone I know wearing my mom's things than a stranger. Do you think you could do that?" Amanda knew Kathrine had very few dresses and probably little else, and hoped the little lady would not take offense.

"I would be pleased to help you with that task. Frankly, I had to leave most of my things in California, so this would be very helpful. I cannot believe my good fortune that you have been sent to enter my life." She reached out to Amanda and the two new friends held each other in a fond caress. They could both feel the relationship changing, however subtly.

On Monday, Amanda went back to work and amid "Welcome back," "How was California?" and other such normal comments, she tried to wade through the mountain of paperwork with ambitions of becoming an avalanche on her desk. She frequently thought of Kathrine and called her twice, each time finding her busy in the closet.

"Oh, Amanda, these clothes are wonderful. I believe your mother and I would have been fast friends. Everything not only fits me like it was made for me, but most are things I would have chosen for myself. I don't know if much at all will make it to the thrift store. I am having just a wonderful time. I hope you don't mind, but I found a small roast in the freezer and I'll prepare it for dinner. Do you have any potatoes?"

The lilt in Kathrine's voice was unmistakable and Amanda lost her last doubt that she had done the right thing. "Look in a dark wooden box in the basement. That's where I keep the potatoes. But please be careful on the stairs. They are wide, and there is a strong handrail, but do take care. I'll look forward to dinner with you." Amanda hung up with a weight off her heart and launched into her paperwork with new vigor.

When Amanda finally completed her last call, the sun was setting low in the west. Her desktop was clean and her conscience was clear. She was looking forward to the dinner Kathrine had promised. Her drive home on Route 400 was slow, but she was moving steadily since she was behind the main rush of traffic. By the time Amanda turned into her driveway and drove into the garage, she was positively salivating for the roast and potatoes. As soon as she opened her car door in the closed garage, the fragrance of the roast wafted through the air and she was twelve years old again. She stood motionless save to inhale slowly, remembering how the kitchen in her childhood home was filled with the same odors.

Amanda opened the door through to the kitchen and stood stock still, frozen by the scene in the kitchen. Her mother was cooking at the stove. The white curls of her head were unruly from the steam of the boiling vegetables. She had a large wooden spoon in her right hand, poking at something in the large aluminum pot. Her housedress was protected by an old apron with ruffled edges, worn pockets, and stains as proof of many delicious meals prepared. "Momma?" Amanda whispered.

"Oh, good, Dear, you're home. Your timing is impeccable. Everything is ready to sit and begin dinner right now." Kathrine looked at Amanda for the first time and saw that she had no color in her face and was trembling visibly.

Kathrine immediately dropped the wooden spoon, hurried over to Amanda and nudged her slowly to the nearest chair.

"What is it, Dear? You look as though you've seen a ghost." The old cliché was not lost on Amanda.

"Kathrine, you look so much like my mother wearing that dress and apron I mistook you for her for a moment. Are you sure you don't have a twin somewhere?" Amanda's bewilderment was confusing to Kathrine.

"Well, if it upsets you so to see these dresses again, I don't want to keep them. To the thrift shop they go tomorrow!"

Amanda knew that was an unnecessary solution and told Kathrine so. But Kathrine made special note to be careful which dresses to wear when Amanda was due home.

"Let's sit and have a nice dinner." Kathrine offered, "Would you care for a glass of wine I found downstairs near the potatoes?"

"Yes, I believe I would!" was Amanda's quick and emphatic reply.

They clinked the wine glasses together in a toast to 'health, wealth, and happiness,' then got down to the business of dinner. The roast was amazing. It had that special quality Amanda remembered from her childhood but had never been able to duplicate. She ate far more that was prudent, promising herself she would visit the exercise room at work tomorrow.

After dinner, they sat and chatted in the front room, or parlor as Kathrine preferred to call it, and soon Amanda's eyes became heavy and she stifled a yawn.

"You must have had a long an arduous day your first day back today. Why don't you retire early and we'll chat more tomorrow." Kathrine was being polite in suggesting Amanda was wearing thin when it was really Kathrine who could hardly keep her eyes open.

The women said goodnight, hugged briefly, and Amanda went up the stairs while Kathrine turned into the little room off the hall. The night passed peacefully under an early Harvest Moon.

Since Monday had been so hectic just playing catch-up, Amanda had a little more time today and began to think of John Gold. She tried to think of who would be the best and quickest source for any information on such a common name. Her mind immediately jumped to a veteran reporter for the station, an old and wizened man who had been around for just ages. He knew everyone; he knew everything, and he would be the first to tell you. So she called him.

"Hi, Norm? This is Amanda Bigelow with WSB. Do you have a minute?"

A deep voice answered back, "For you, Honey, anytime. Whatcha need?"

"Well, I'm trying to find someone and don't have much to start with. You are just so good at this kind of thing, I didn't even bother to call anyone else." Amanda knew puffing up Norm's ego couldn't hurt her cause.

"OK, Babe, you don't have to blow any more smoke. Tell me whatcha got."

"His name is John Gold, he has been in Roswell for a while and very recently moved to the Buckhead area, I don't know where. I have an old phone number which has been disconnected. He's about 50, tall, lanky, wears his hair long and in a pony-tail in the back. He seems to like gaudy jewelry. His mother told me he wears several large gold necklaces and at least one earring. I get the impression he isn't the most responsible person, so may not hold a job too long. He has a car, but I don't know what kind. He was born in Northeastern Pennsylvania in a small town the name of which I don't know. Apparently several generations have lived there quite a while. That's about it. Sorry it's not too much." Amanda wished fervently she had asked more questions about John Gold and had more to give Norm.

"OK, Sweetie, that's really a lot more information than I usually get. I'll see what I can find out and call you back. OK to call at home?"

"I'd prefer you didn't. His mother is a guest at my house and this is news I would rather have a chance to filter, if you know what I mean."

Norm told her, "Ten-four. I'll leave you a voice mail if you're out of the office."

Amanda thanked him and knew the information was in good hands. If anyone could come up with anything concrete, it would be Norm. He had a well deserved reputation for finding the impossible.

Another day behind her, dinner waiting, and the odor in the garage was pork chops today. But this time Amanda took a moment to prepare herself for the visual shock she expected to encounter. She was not disappointed, though Kathrine had taken special care to comb her hair differently, and not use the apron – or the wooden spoon.

"Smells good." Amanda raised the lid and sniffed the steam curling from the pot. "What is it?"

"Stuffed pork chops." A proud Kathrine bragged. "A recipe my John used to love. He has been on my mind the last couple of days. Today I tried calling the last number I had for him and it was disconnected."

Though Amanda knew this, she acted surprised. She didn't want Kathrine to know of her research. At least not just yet.

They sat and savored the moist stuffed pork chops, butternut squash, and a pungent salad with cucumbers and onions marinated in sour cream, sugar and vinegar. Amanda could barely walk after she cleaned her plate.

"I can't do this too often, Kathrine, I'll be big as a blimp! But it was so good. Thank you for a wonderful meal."

Kathrine smiled, "And thank you for the good conversation and all you've done for me. As soon as I locate John, I'll be out from underfoot."

"Don't be silly." Amanda admonished. "You are welcome here as long as you want to stay. You are such good company."

They said their goodnights and slept like angels.

Early to work the next day, Amanda pushed the blinking button for her voice mail. "Hey, Girlie. This is Norm. I have some info on that John Gold." Her heart beating quickly, she sat on the edge of her chair with pencil in hand to take notes, paying rapt attention to the recording. Norm continued, "It ain't good news. He was killed in a car wreck a week ago. Single car crash. Hit a big tree. His alcohol level was three times the limit and he had a pocket full of meth, enough to have him arrested as a dealer if he'd lived. He had a wrap sheet half a mile long so he was no stranger to the law. Anyway, give me a call. There's more news I don't want to leave on voicemail. Catch ya later, Babe. Bye."

Amanda sank into her chair. How was she ever going to tell that dear Kathrine her son not only had died, but under such unsavory circumstances. Her day was ruined. She pushed papers from one side of her desk to the other and then back again. She divided the sheets into three stacks and then shuffled them back into one big pile. She tried to type an article on which she had been working but it was like typing with her feet. The spell-check on her word processor was going nuts. She gave up that project and decided to try to call Norm.

"Hey, Sweets." To Amanda's surprise, Norm answered on the second ring.

"How did you know it was me?" Amanda wondered.

"Caller ID on my new phone. It tells me the name and number of the caller. Pretty cool if you ask me. Anyway, you're calling about the dead guy?"

Amanda grimaced at the pragmatism of Norm's question. "Yes, what other information do you have?"

"You're gonna love this. Along with all the bad stuff he had on him, he also had some pretty expensive jewelry, a two karat diamond earring for one thing! And get this: over $150,000 in cash. The cops can't tie any of this stuff to a robbery or any-thing else illegal, so it goes to next of kin with proper proof."

Amanda was just stunned. This was like a good news/bad news joke. "Hey, Lady, you're son's dead but you're rich." She thanked Norm for the quick work and acknowledged that she owed him a favor for his efforts. Now all she could do was mull over in her mind the information she had just received.

And wonder the best way to give the information to the woman who had so quickly become a part of her life.

The work on Amanda's desk could have been written in Chi-nese for all the sense she was making of it today, so she told her editor she had some tips to check outside the office and would be back tomorrow morning. On her way home, she avoided Route 400 as it was reported jammed. A semi truck had lost its load of little stuffed toys, Beanie Babies, which were extremely popular with the younger set. The crazy drivers were stopping right in the middle of the highway to grab up as many of the treasures as they could. That would be a while to clear!

The smaller roads winding through the grand and gracious old Atlanta neighborhoods gave Amanda the mental breather she needed. She decided that Kathrine was an intelligent woman and had shown a strong constitution in the face of the adversities thrust upon her lately. Amanda thought open honesty and forthrightness was the best way to convey the bad news; Kathrine deserved no less.

Having made that decision, Amanda breathed a sigh of relief, re-entered Route 400 above the Beanie Baby fiasco, so she made good time home.

"My, you're early today. Is everything all right?" With that question from Kathrine, Amanda had the perfect entrance for her information.

"No, Kathrine, it isn't. Would you come and sit with me at the kitchen table?"

They sat, Kathrine's face one wrinkled question mark, and Amanda began with a shaky breath. "I had one of my good friends at work see if he could locate your son."

Kathrine looked expectant and said, "Did he find him?"

"Well, yes. But I'm afraid the news isn't too good."

"Is he hurt? Where is he, I'll go right away if you'll drive me."

"No, Kathrine, he isn't hurt. I'm afraid it is much worse than that."

After a pause during which all color drained from Kathrine's face, she whispered, "He's dead, isn't he?"

Amanda nodded, and the small dishtowel Kathrine held in her lap became a sea of knots and the tears from her old blue eyes were fresh and plentiful. Amanda gave the woman a few moments before she spoke.

Kathrine broke the silence when she asked, "What happened? Did he suffer?"

"No, his death was instant. My information is that he was driving at a great rate of speed and hit a tree. No one else was involved, either persons or vehicles."

This piece of news seemed to ease the pain on the old lady's face, though the tears did not stop. "Was John running from the police?"

This question startled Amanda and she was quite taken aback hearing it. "I don't know that, Kathrine. But there is some other information, some bad and some good. When John had the accident he had been drinking and his blood alcohol level was quite high."

"How high?"

"Three times the legal limit."

Kathrine shook her head and used the wrinkled dishtowel to pat her cheeks dry. "Is that all?"

Amanda couldn't help but think that this woman knew her son well and his habits were not surprising. "No, Kathrine, he had some methamphetamines in his pocket which, had they been found on him when he was alive, would have been enough to arrest him as a dealer."

"Well, I'm not surprised at all about that." Kathrine pulled a face. "I warned him and warned him that he would get into trouble with that stuff."

The younger woman could barely contain her surprise at these last statements. Kathrine had left the impression that, though a little irresponsible, John was a good person. "My friend discovered other news that may be of interest to you."

"OK, what's that? Let's hear the whole thing!" Kathrine's demeanor was curt and disgusted, so Amanda tread carefully with her next statements.

"You had mentioned John wore jewelry, quite a bit if it?" This was posed as a question to defray the negativity of the last bit of conversation.

"Yes, he always did like the gaudy big fat gold necklaces. Why?"

"When the police recovered his remains from the vehicle accident, he was wearing the necklaces. Also an expensive watch and other gold bracelets. He did have an earring in one ear, as you had mentioned, and it was a two karat solitaire diamond."

Kathrine tried to whistle but her old lips wouldn't form the proper shape and all that emerged was a meaningful swish of air.

"That's not all, John also had over $150,000 cash in his possession. None of these items can be traced to a crime of any kind, so they go to the next of kin."

"Next of kin?"

"Yes, Kathrine. It all goes to you if you have proof he is your son."

The first hint of a smile crossed Kathrine's crooked mouth as she said, "One of the few things I have in my small valise is his birth certificate and an old birth certificate of mine."

"That should do it. But you will need to go to the Cobb County Morgue and identify the body. Do you feel up to that?" Amanda didn't think so but needed to let Kathrine know it was necessary.

Kathrine's white curls bobbed as she shook her head, "I'm not up to that now. I need to digest this news and accept that which I knew was the inevitable." She paused and looked at Amanda. "Is there a church nearby?"

"There is a Catholic church two blocks away and a Methodist church right on the corner. Do you want to go now?"

Kathrine's blue eyes gazed unseeing at Amanda for a moment and then Kathrine chose the Methodist church. They went to the car and made the short drive.

"Would you like for me to come in with you?" Amanda knew what the answer would be, but asked the question anyway.

"No, Dear. But if you could help me out of you car. It is so high off the ground my short little legs don't work too well."

Amanda rounded the car, got the walker from the back seat, opened the door and gave Kathrine the aid she needed to land squarely on the pavement. Amanda watched Kathrine navigate the few steps and disappear into the darkness of the sanctuary.

The sun was just dipping behind the trees, casting long shadows over the stone portico of the old church when Kathrine came slowly out of the church, the minister at her side, hand on her shoulder. They were smiling at each other and Kathrine's countenance was softened and more relaxed than Amanda had seen since that first walk down the aisle of the airplane. The two old people parted, speaking words to each other which were lost in the evening shade, and Kathrine headed for the car. Amanda jumped out to open the door and help her friend up into her seat.

Nearly back to the house, Kathrine was the first to speak. "John is with his Maker now. I hope he is at peace. The minister's name is John, too. Isn't that a coincidence? We prayed for a long time and read passages in the Bible that were such a comfort to me. I may go back to that church on Sunday. Would you take me?"

"Of course. I'm glad you had a good meeting with Reverend John. I've known him for quite a while. He is a very nice man and the congregation adores him." Amanda couldn't convey the relief she felt for her friend, and she was so pleased Reverend John had been in the church at this time. "Well, I don't know about you, but I'm hungry. Could you do with a bowl of clam chowder?"

A laughing voice said, "I could do with a bucket of it! Do you have some?"

"No, but there is a seafood restaurant, Norman's Landing, that makes the best clam chowder south of the north pole.....or so they claim. And it is really pretty good. A nice salad and warm bowl of chowder should help chase away your blues." Amanda was hopeful that Kathrine's lighter mood would not evaporate any time soon. "Well, let's go find some clams!"

Kathrine was more than ready. She was just beginning to realize it had been hours since her last meal. The news of John's death and the conditions surrounding it had held her mind and body in check. She needed to unwind.

The friends rode silently for the short ride to Cumming, and opted for valet parking under the threat of rain later in the evening. Amanda noticed that Kathrine left the walker in the back seat and waited to take Amanda's arm to enter the establishment.

It was a pretty place. There was a lot of dark wood giving it an old and comfortable feeling. Areas of bright light were interspersed among small tables with softer, more intimate ambience. A large bar in the far corner pushed laughter and happy chatter throughout the restaurant without being obnoxious. Kathrine immediately like the rooms with their different nautical personalities. A pretty young woman in low slung trousers asked them to follow and rolled her hips in such a way that Amanda and Kathrine looked at each other and suppressed a giggle.

Seated at a nice quiet table by a window looking out onto the manicured lawn and garden area, they read the huge menus with tiny print to judge the offerings of the establishment. Since they had both decided on salad and chowder on the short ride from the house, the choices were a non-issue. They did, however, each order a glass of wine, Amanda a chardonnay and Kathrine asked for Chablis.

"My mother liked Chablis." Amanda reminisced. "I don't really recall her ever drinking much else with a nice dinner. She even cooked with it in certain dishes."

"I'll bet one of them was an Alfredo sauce for pasta." Kathrine challenged.

"You are absolutely right. Ah, here are the salads already."

Kathrine was amazed at the size of the bowls. "I'll never be able to eat all of this!"

"Then we will ask for a 'doggie bag'."

"And take it home? Will it last till tomorrow?" Kathrine's furrowed brows were an indication of her aversion to wasting food.

Amanda assured her, "Yes, and so will the chowder if you can't finish that. And if you think this bowl is big, wait until you see the soup bowls!"

The salads were crispy, fresh and delicious, so conversation paused.

Eventually Kathrine brought up the subject that had been hanging in the air. "When will I have to go identify John and make arrangements for him?"

"Whenever you are ready. Honestly, the quicker the better. Things like this are best not left to fester. We can go tomorrow if you feel up to it." Amanda knew the longer Kathrine waited the more difficult it would become.

Kathrine capitulated. "If you can make the arrangements, I will take care of it tomorrow. But you must come with me. I just could not do it alone."

"I would never consider your going unaccompanied." Amanda tried to put the worried woman at peace. "I'll make a call to the Cobb County Coroner early and see if we can't get down there by noon."

They completed what they could of the salad and wonderful clam chowder, and each carried a large bag of leftovers to the car. It had rained while they were eating, so Amanda was glad to have chosen the valet parking.

Upon returning to the house, they deposited the treasures from the restaurant into the refrigerator, gave each other a quick good-night hug, and walked with their own thoughts to their rooms, the next day heavy on each mind.

Amanda called in to her editor and explained what she needed to do today and was given immediate permission and a genuine offer of any help she might need. She graciously declined and thanked her editor for being so understanding.

"OK, Kathrine, are you ready to go?" Amanda was gathering

her purse, car keys, sunglasses and such as she asked, but when she turned around to see if the elder lady was ready, Amanda could not avoid a quick and harsh intake of breath. Before her stood her mother: the favorite floral organdy dress, shoes a matching though muted umber with short heals and rounded toes, square purse with a short handle the same leather as the shoes. Kathrine even carried her short white kid gloves she had worn on the plane. Amanda's mother had always felt gloves were necessary to complete an elegant ensemble.

Amanda's vision blurred when she noticed the little hat, fitted close to Kathrine's head and nearly hidden by the curls. It was the small plain hat her mother had painstakingly covered with tiny and colorful parakeet feathers, each one stitched individually by hand. Amanda's parents had tried to breed parakeets many years ago and the only thing the little birds made was feathers. So Amanda's mother had saved them on this hat.

Amanda wavered and had to sit down. Her knees were becoming increasingly shaky; it was in keeping with the throbbing of her heart.

"Dear?" a concerned Kathrine rushed to Amanda's side. "Are you alright? You look as though you've seen a ghost!"

Amanda knew the blood had drained from her face, and managed a small smile at the unwitting irony of the words. "Yes, Kathrine, I'm just fine. I just this instant remembered a deadline I have for noon today." She tried to look pensive and said, "But I'm sure my editor will cover it for me. The article is nearly completed. Why don't we get started, it's a bit of a drive through heavy traffic this time of day."

They entered the garage and Amanda had a surprise for Kathrine: a small step stool. It was just high enough to afford Kathrine a comfortable step from the floor to the stool and from the stool into the vehicle. "What a wonderful idea. Thank you."

Amanda put the little stool behind the front seat with the walker, walked around her car and climbed in. The short drive through the neighborhoods was always beautiful, and a peaceful mental preparation for the chaos of Route 400 traffic.

In spite of the heavy commuter traffic, they arrived at their appointment time, and the desk sergeant announced their presence to the County Coroner. Both Amanda and Kathrine were surprised when a pretty blonde woman about 45 came through the double doors. Her flowing white lab coat was embroidered with block letters "Coroner" and smaller letters beneath named her Leah.

Leah approached the two women, shook Amanda's hand then Kathrine's and said, "You must be Kathrine Gold."

After a nod of acknowledgment, Leah continued, "First, Mrs. Gold, let me express my condolences for your loss," and after a polite pause, continued, "I can see a family resemblance. Though your son was killed instantly in the crash, the airbag kept his facial features in tact. He was a handsome young man. Please come this way with me please." And she motioned through the double doors and to the right.

A very apprehensive Kathrine took Amanda's arm and her blue eyes were searching for some reassurance. Leah offered a modicum of it when she asked Kathrine if she would rather view her son in person or through a video camera on a television set.

"Did you say he was not disfigured?" was Kathrine's first question.

"His fatal disfigurements are well hidden beneath the sterile cloths covering his body. Your son's upper body, face and head are fine. The choice is yours completely. Either method is acceptable for legal identification."

After a pause and a squeeze of Amanda's hand, Kathrine told

Leah she would prefer to see him in person. She said she felt she could more easily say her goodbyes.

"Then give me just a moment to prepare him for you." And Leah disappeared through yet another set of double doors.

In the blink of an eye, it seemed, Leah opened one of the doors and motioned for Kathrine to enter.

"May Amanda be with me?" Kathrine had come to depend so on her young friend.

"Of course, but she may not touch or say anything. This will all be recorded on video for the files." Leah was very businesslike, and this was an appreciated level of professionalism.

The three women walked into the stark white room, felt the chill in the air and heard the strange quiet. There was a gurney a short walk to the left and Leah went to it and around to the other side.

"Are you ready? This may be more difficult than you expect." Leah was trying to prepare the older woman for what she knew was going to be a traumatic experience.

Kathrine simply nodded and kept her hand in Amanda's and

her eyes on the drape of the cloth over the head. Leah took the top of the cloth with both hands, folded it slowly down past the hairline, then the second fold revealed John's full face.

Kathrine's knees buckled slightly and Amanda grabbed her around the waist. "It is John. That is my son." Kathrine leaned into Amanda for the support which her own legs had abandoned.

Quickly Leah recovered the head and ushered the women back to the warmer hallway. There were benches lining the walls and Kathrine immediately took advantage of the nearest one. She was shaken far beyond her expectations. Knowing this event was eminent, Kathrine had spent the sleepless night before trying to visualize what she might see of her beloved only child, her dear son. Regardless of the unsavory factions of the law in which he had been involved, her mothers' love never abated. Knowing he was dead and seeing him in that condition were two incomparable experiences.

Amanda gave the older woman a few moments to herself before she sat on the bench. Leah had returned to the cold room behind the double doors.

Kathrine reached for Amanda's hand and clutched it as though never to release it. They sat solemnly, Amanda sensing

Kathrine needed quiet time to assemble her thoughts and composure. The two women jumped slightly as Leah burst again through the wide doors and asked Kathrine, "Would you like to go verify and collect your son's personal effects? The desk sergeant has some time now."

Glad for a change in subject, however minor, Kathrine gave a wan smile and nodded. Still clutching Amanda's hand as though it were life itself, the three women started down the long corridor.

"Sarge, this is Mrs. Gold, she is John Gold's mother. I under-stand you have some of his personal effects?" Leah, already knowing the answer, went through the formal motions to feed the large ego of the sergeant.

"Sure do. Right back there on the shelf. Need to see some ID, first." He was addressing Leah. "She could be anybody after this stuff, ya know."

Kathrine stiffened at this unkind statement, released Amanda's hand, reached into her purse and staunchly pushed John's birth certificate and her own birth certificate through the window and under the rude sergeant's nose. And in her best forceful voice asked, "Will *these* do, young man? And you need not be so impolite."

Amanda had to turn her head to hide her involuntary smile. She had never heard such a harsh tone of voice coming from this gentle woman.

The rotund sergeant with the red nose and ears had the good grace to appear contrite as he apologized softly. He examined the documents, nodded his head and returned the items to Kathrine. He then left the window to blend into an amazing array of shelves and boxes. The women could hear him pushing boxes around and mumbling an unpleasant expletive periodically, but he shortly returned with a cardboard box about one foot high, one foot wide, and two feet deep.

The name "John Gold" was printed in large block letters, along with a date and some smaller indistinguishable printing beneath. The sergeant pushed some papers and a pen through the little opening in the bars separating him from the outside world and told Kathrine to sign.

Since Kathrine's dander was already up, she looked the large man in the eye and said, "Not until I read every word. I'm not sure exactly what you would have me sign, Young Man. I do not like your demeanor and therefore you have not earned my trust."

This minor explosion from the little person even brought a smile from Leah. The sergeant, however, turned red as a beet and hung his head.

After a cursory glance at the papers, Kathrine handed them to Amanda, who glanced at each page, then handed them back saying, "Kathrine, I think these are just a receipt for the goods in the box. And certifying the documents you presented are true and correct. They look fine."

"Thank you." Kathrine said and with all the military bearing she could muster, she placed the papers on the counter in front of the now quiet sergeant and signed where indicated.

She handed the papers back, and wondered how the box was going to fit through the small opening, when the sergeant produced a set of keys, fitted one into an obscure lock, and a large portion of the bars swung outward. The sergeant pushed the box through the opening and Amanda reached for it. When she lifted it off the counter she nearly dropped it. It was much heavier than she had anticipated, but she repositioned her hold and thanked the sergeant for his help.

"Little Lady," the sergeant called softly after Kathrine, "I didn't mean to be so bad on you. I'm sorry. I'm sorry you lost your son, too."

"Thank you for that. Good day." And Kathrine and Amanda left Leah standing by the sergeant as they made their exit from the building.

Back home in Amanda's kitchen, the still closed box on the table, Kathrine pondered, "What do you suppose is in this box; it weighs a ton! Should I open it?"

"It's your box. You can leave it sitting here on the table if you like, or I can take it to your room."

"No. I think I want to get into it here, with you beside me. Will you bring me the scissors, please?" And short work was made of the tape which sealed the top of the box to the bottom.

Kathrine took a deep breath, closed her eyes for a moment, then wiggled the top from the box, revealing the contents for the first time.

"Oh, my God!" Kathrine and Amanda could only stare at what they saw. Cash. Loose cash and a lot of it. Mostly $100 bills and they filled the box nearly to the top.

The women started to assemble piles and count the money when Amanda's fingers struck something hard. She dug down through the bills and pulled out a thick and heavy gold chain. At the sight of this, Kathrine sank immediately into the chair beside her as Amanda held it out to her.

"That was John's. He wore it all the time. I asked him once where he got such an expensive thing and he told me he had won a sales contest. I believed him. Now I know what kind of sales he was in and I know it was no contest!" Though her words were rebuking, her fingers caressed the long metal rope as she would have touched a baby.

Amanda found 6 more such necklaces, a large Rolex watch, three thick gold bracelets and one silver one. The diamond earring was in a small plastic bag, as was a gold ring with a huge red stone surrounded by diamonds. "Probably a ruby, Amanda. John was born in July."

Several hours later, the cash counted, neatly wrapped and to-gether with rubber bands, Kathrine was the new owner of $597,860.

"I just can't believe it! Look at all this money! I don't know what to do with it. This morning I had $35.00 in my purse and now......." Kathrine was befuddled with her sudden good for-tune. ".....now I just don't know what to do with all this." She thought for a moment, "A good pair of walking shoes, I really need a pair. And a nice purse. And some dresses for church." Kathrine immediately looked apologetic towards Amanda and said, "That isn't to say I haven't enjoyed your mother's dresses. There are several I would love to keep if you'll allow. But I have not been shopping for new clothes in so many years."

Amanda could but smile at the utter glee of the little lady. "Well, maybe we should consider getting your fortune off the kitchen table and into a bank. Do you have one now?"

"No, I haven't had enough money to have a bank account in, oh, I don't know how long. Do you have a good bank?"

Amanda answered in the affirmative and it was decided that first thing tomorrow they would take care of that. Amanda also recommended a safe deposit box for the jewelry.

"I've never had a safe deposit box. I've always thought it made one sound so grand. And now it's me." Kathrine just sat there, looking at the array of riches before her and simply smiled. "And I do feel so grand. So very grand.'

"Maybe, after I have nice clothes to wear, I could return to my home town. I married the high school bully and left for the 'Big City' of Forrest City. I got pregnant right away, and Richie ran out the door as soon as I told him. I couldn't go back home, I was too embarrassed. But I was lucky enough to find a convent who took in young girls in my situation. I was even lucky enough to find a job good enough to be able to keep my baby, my John. A lot of people had to give their children up because they just couldn't afford to feed them. It was awful!" She shook her head at the hurtful memories.

"But no more!" Kathrine brightened. "Those people in Pleasant Mount will surely know I did not fail in life. That will be so splendid."

Amanda took a short quick breath. "Did you say Pleasant Mount?"

"Yes, why?"

"Pennsylvania?"

"Yes, Dear, why? What's the matter?"

"My mother said she was born in Pleasant Mount. In July of 1927."

"July what? The 28th?"

Amanda's mind was running in circles. "Yes, July 28th. She was born in Pleasant Mount but told me her family had to move to Binghamton, NY to find work. Pleasant Mount had little industry other than a fish hatchery at the bottom of the hill. Her mother told her they lived in a house at the edge of town looking down the hill. They did not want to leave, but had no choice. They opened a delicatessen in downtown Binghamton and lived there in a big stone house until they both died "

Kathrine hung on every word. She asked Amanda if she had a copy of her mother's birth certificate. Amanda was confused by that, but said she kept it with the death certificate and other important papers of her mom's. "Would you go and get it, please?"

Of course Amanda complied, rising immediately from the kitchen chair and turning down the hall.

Kathrine opened her own purse and extracted the papers she had shown to the sergeant this afternoon as proof of next of kin to John. One of the papers had been John's birth certificate; the other had been her own. She inspected it very carefully, but through the wrinkles from years of folding the names were difficult to read. It said: Mother's name, Norah Caffery, Father's name Otis Caffery, date of birth: July 28, 1927, Order of birth, 1 of 2. And was signed by the delivering MD and attending nurse in Pleasant Mount, Pennsylvania. In all these years, Kathrine had never seen the order of birth, 1 of 2. She was a twin. She was awestruck.

About that time, Amanda returned with an old paper in her hand. She saw the color had drained from Kathrine's face and knelt quickly at her side.

"What is it? Are you alright?" Amanda knew how much mental pressure the older woman had experienced today and was fearful for her health.

With no words, Kathrine handed her birth certificate to Amanda and pointed to the area of importance. Amanda read Kathrine's, then quickly inspected her own. Amanda's birth certificate was filled out with the same words: Mother's name, Norah Caffery, Father's name Otis Caffery, date of birth: July 28, 1927, child's name Kathleen Martha, order of birth, 2 of 2. And was signed by the same delivering MD and attending nurse in Pleasant Mount, Pennsylvania. The only differences in the documents were times of deliveries (Kathrine was 13 minutes ahead of the second birth), and the names of the infants.

They were Kathrine Margaret Caffery and Kathleen Martha Caffery. This dear sweet woman who had come so softly into Amanda's life and over whom Amanda felt so protective was her own mother's twin sister. She was Amanda's aunt.

In the back of Amanda's mind formed the recollection of children being given to families of more fortunate means, and began to realize this is what must have happened to the tiny twin girls.   Kathrine remained with the family in Pleasant Mount while Kathleen's new family had taken her to Binghamton, NY. Neither girl had been told they had a sister; Kathrine had been told a child had died and Kathleen apparently had been reared an only child.

The realization that the same blood coursed through their veins came to both women simultaneously, and they embraced in a long, strong, tearful and delighted hug.   Then they began to laugh – then to giggle. Their emotions were so high and so uncapturable at that moment that all they could do was to giggle. Amanda raised herself from the floor and brought Kathrine up with her into a little dance around the kitchen table. What a wonder this was to both of them.

"I guess I call you Aunt Kathrine now!" Amanda's smile had been so broad for so long that she felt slight cramps at her cheeks.   She gently placed her new-found aunt back in the chair by the table and began to put the treasure back into it's plain box. We'll take care of this tomorrow, but for tonight, I want to know all about your life.

The next few hours fluttered by on wings of angels of history as the women recalled details, Kathrine of her own life and Amanda recollecting her mother's young life.

It was such a magic time, both women were reluctant to end the conversation and retire to bed. But hearing the hall clock chime midnight nudged the decision along.

They both rose early and met in the kitchen with a big hug.

"Good morning, Aunt Kathrine." A huge grin accompanied the happy greeting.

"And a good morning to you, my dear niece." Every wrinkle on Katherine's face was smiling.

They shared a cup of coffee, and Amanda was the first to break the peaceful silence. "Kathrine, this has been a roller coaster for you, I know. But I must ask you this now, though you may answer later."

"What is it, Dear." The white brows furrowed over the crystal blue eyes.

"I want you to stay here with me. Even before the discovery of our true relationship, I had grown to feel so protective toward you, and a spark of a deep and abiding friendship was growing. I was planning to ask you if you would consider remaining with me. I have plenty of room, you would never want for anything, you could even....." Amanda was working up an unnecessary plea.

"Oh, my dear, dear girl. I, too, have a strong affection for you. You took me into your home as a stranger and never once made me feel like a lesser person. I enjoy your company and love cooking and doing for you." Smiling Kathrine said, "I planned to ask if you would rent that room to me."

"No. You don't rent to relatives. The room is yours to use as long as you like."

The glisten in Kathrine's eyes sealed the agreement and the two women sipped their coffee in companionable silence.

After dressing, Amanda helped Kathrine into the car with the little stool, tucked it into the back seat, and fastened herself behind the steering wheel.

Well, Auntie," Amanda said lightly, "Shall we be on our way to introduce the town's newest lady of means to the president of the bank?"

It took a moment for the thought to register with Kathrine, but then she grinned and, with a wave of her little gloved hand said, "But of course, My Dear, but of course."

They backed slowly down the driveway, turned toward the center of the southern Georgia town and disappeared into the fine morning mist.

End

Rewards

Author's Note:

This story is the product of a writing contest I entered in the Summer of 2006. The rules of the contest were that the story be an original, fifteen hundred words or less, never published (no problem there!), and begin with the words: "The clerk looked …"

The winner of the contest would be published in the fall Quarterly issue in September.

So I sat down at my keyboard, wrote what I thought was a suitable short story, and promptly had to cut about 300 words and one whole character from it!

Confidently, I typed up my title page, wrote out my check for the three dollario Readers' Fee, and sent my precious manuscript out.

As of this date, the September issue of the magazine has been on the stand for several months, and I haven't found my story in any of the issues I've seen.

Oh, well, maybe better luck next time. I, of course, think it is wonderful and just cannot understand why it wouldn't win even honorable mention.

I hope you enjoy reading it.

<u>Rewards</u>

The clerk looked into the oxidized grey bucket of liquid yuk, swished the glob of cotton snakes around in it, wrung the filthy water out and slapped the mop to the floor. She scowled and mumbled 'Sailor Words' (her son's label of his late father's language) as she tried to erase the black heel marks and brown coffee stains from the tiles.

Bringing her pudgy frame upright, Anna was standing in the center of a small office, crammed with mismatched desks, all pushed together so closely she had to move sideways between most of them. Bending to mop the floors was a challenge to be sure. She was most particular around her own desk. And during the day when she sat and worked there, she was careful to not spill liquid or drop a marker, and she wore shoes that left no dark lines.

She propped the mop against the desk behind hers, rested a moment in her familiar chair, and lovingly dusted the picture of her two kids. She brought the small frame to her face and lightly kissed the image of each of them. Her round cheeks puffed upward with an adoring smile at the images.

"Ah, well," she sighed. "This is all going to be worth it when you two are doctors or lawyers and famous and rich!" She swiveled in her chair to begin dusting the top of the desk behind hers. It was sparsely covered, arranged precisely, and decorated only by a little metal pitcher holding one tiny red ribbon rose.

"This is so pretty," she thought. "It looks like gold. Sorta like those old pitchers in the fairy tales I used to read the kids." Again she sighed, and playing along with her own fantasy thoughts, she stood, looked upward, closed her eyes, and sheltered the little vessel gently within her rough and calloused hands. "I wish I may, I wish I might, have this wish I wish tonight." She chanted the childhood mantra softly. She smiled, shaking her head in mild self-admonishment, and moved to put the little pitcher back. Then shrugged, regained her soft hold on the container, pursed her lips and fancied, "OK. OK, I wish I could get some relief from all this work and be able to spend more time with my kids."

They were good kids, but still kids. Her 17 year old son, Stuart, had already received several scholarship offers from prestigious colleges around the country due to his exceptional work on the high school debating team. This was beyond Anna, she didn't even understand most of the subjects of discussion, let alone his arguments.

At fourteen, her daughter Susie was attracting attention and building an expanding portfolio with the local modeling agencies. Anna's night job was earning extra income to finance a trip for her and Susie to meet personally with agents in Charleston.

Anna glanced again at the pretty little golden pitcher, threw it a rueful smile and returned to her distasteful work.

The next morning, Anna dressed for her office job, packed her cleaning clothes and lunch in a little satchel and set it by the front door before waking her teenagers.

"Stuart? It's 7:30, get up! You're going to be late for school." Anna knocked softly on his door and heard the muted tippy-tap of his computer keyboard.

"OK, Mom. I'll be right out." The deep young voice confirmed he was awake.

"You wait too long to do your homework. You should have finished it last night." Anna's rebuke was lost to Stuart when she turned towards Susie's door. As Anna reached up to knock, the door opened quickly and she nearly knocked on her daughter's head.

At 14, Susie stood nearly a foot taller than her mother, was thin and graceful as a willow, her face fresh with discovering the excitement of life. Susie was very photogenic; smiling, unsmiling, even scowling, the camera loved her face. She had begun to bring some income into the house from her modeling jobs, but Anna insisted it go into a college fund. "Beauty doesn't last forever." She would say.

Confirming both teenagers were conscious, Anna circled back to the kitchen to pour herself coffee and deposit frozen waffles into the toaster. Susie was first into the kitchen catching the hot waffles as they popped from the toaster. She slathered them with butter and drowned them in syrup before consuming them quickly.

"Avoiding that fat and sugar will help your career!" Anna cautioned.

"Mom! All kids eat like this!"

"Not kids trying to land jobs with the biggest modeling agencies in Charleston!"

"OK. OK. I'll just have four this morning. Happy?"

Anna could only smile. What ancestry blessed her with this tall and beautiful girl sitting at her kitchen counter and her genius son? Daily Anna thanked The Lord for her two wonderful children.

Stuart was still missing from breakfast, and Anna yelled again, "Stu – you're going to be late. Turn that computer off. Now!"

Stuart's door burst open and he rushed out, buttoning his shirt with one hand and balancing books and a pile of papers in the other. "Sorry, Mom. I had this thing I thought was due Wednesday, but it's today and I had to finish." His hair was ruffled, his cheeks flushed and he had missed a button on his shirt. Anna was watching her baby become a man in front of her very eyes.

Stuart fought Susie for the two fresh waffles blasting out of the toaster. He won, and soon butter and syrup were flying.

"I need to get some fruit!" Silently Anna thought, then aloud, "OK, Guys, I'm going. Lock the door and have a good day. Call me when you get home from school. Love you both."

"Love you, too, Mom." From Susie.

"Me, too, but I'll be a little late this afternoon. I'm meeting with, uh, a guidance counselor." Stuart fumbled as Anna closed the door behind her.

At her desk, Anna worked on her software project, pecking the keyboard as her fingers tried to keep up with her mind. She couldn't spell or write well, but she knew how to make a computer purr and write code for any application.

"Good morning." The greeting came from behind her.

She smiled at the gentleman, hoping he wouldn't notice a disturbance of his desk after her antics with the little metal pitcher. "The same to you. How's it going?"

"I feel I'm beginning to fit in." He said with a tic of his bald head.

"I felt the same way at first. The sensation will pass." Anna turned back to her own work. Soon the hum of his computer joined the quiet harmonics of the office.

Half a year passed, graduation was nearing for Stuart; his excitement was palpable. He had chosen Clemson University for its excellence in debate. The team had taken National Honors in last year's contest, now hoping to retain the honor this year. With the campus close, the family could be together weekends.

Susie and Anna had finally saved the funding for a week in Charleston to pursue Susie's dream. They were going to the city after Stuart's graduation.

One evening Anna lumbered down the hall, exhausted from a long week with extra hours, Susie close behind her. Anna's software was becoming of particular interest to the managing partners meaning added pressure and more hours. But her janitorial duties couldn't be ignored, so Susie had stepped in to help.

As Susie opened the apartment door for the exhausted Anna, Stuart jumped out of his chair in the living room and ran to grab his mother in a hug. He was grinning so hard his ears nearly disappeared. He let go of Anna and reached for Susie, who backed away suspiciously.

"What on earth??" Anna was startled by the show of emotion from her normally subdued son.

Stuart shook an envelope at her. "Mom! Mom! Look at this!"

Anna opened the envelope, unfolded the letter and a smaller paper fell to the floor. Susie reached down for it and screamed as she read it.

"Mom! MOM! It's a check for $25,000! It's for Stu! Look!" And she handed it to Anna.

"What?...." Anna was baffled. She tried to read the letter as Susie jabbered and Stuart stood stoically with arms crossed, waiting. The letter was from a publishing company in New York requesting an exclusive contract for his writing, and a retainer of $25,000 for his first book if Stuart agreed. They had re-viewed the first three chapters and were very impressed with the new writer.

"When did you do this?" Anna asked.

"Usually early mornings." Stuart told her. "I never thought any-thing would come of it. There was this contest in a magazine. I entered it. I won." He shuffled his feet. "Do you want to read it?"

"Yes! Of course!! Where is it?"

As she settled into a comfortable chair, Stuart handed her a stack of papers she and began to read: "The clerk looked..."

End

My
Dear
Aunt
Sally

My Dear Aunt Sally

"You think *you've* got a weird family – wait till I tell you what I found out about mine!" Anne's wide girth was perched on a little green parlor chair, the cushion of which was all but hidden by the folds of her skirts. Her shiny brown hair flew about her face in the spring breeze and she fought to keep it behind her ears and out of her mouth as she spoke. Her blue eyes*** shined with a twinkle twenty years her junior.

Anne had met two of her good friends for lunch, and they had shared a sparse luncheon consisting of tiny cucumber sandwiches cut into triangles with no crust, little crackers with scant amounts of cheese perched upon them, and one caper for decoration. They had decided to take a break from fast food and plentiful buffets to treat themselves at a little tea house about a half hour out of town. All three, especially Anne, had deep belly laughs and found humor in everything. This fact was not lost on the wait staff of the upper-crust teahouse nor any of the surrounding guests.

They were having a ball, but the waiter charged with their table gave them disapproving sideways glances whenever the trio dissolved in mirth. The very size of the plates and the oh, so delicate floral china teacup was enough to start the bunch of them dissolving into a fit of giggles.

Marie was the eldest of the three. She was, as she said, pushing 70, looking 60, feeling 40, and acting 20. Her hair was nearly pure white, and she wore it very short and in a spiked style. She had huge round deep red glasses which perched near the end of her nose, allowing her to peer over the tops for the most raucous effect. She was tiny, barely five feet, almost 100 pounds, but feisty as could be. And she ate more than the other two combined!

The third member of this little clan was Frances, or Frankie to her friends. If you took Anne and Marie, put them in a sack and shook them up, Frankie would fall out. Mid-60's, she very recently retired from a government job she had held for 27 years. The fact that it took 2 people to replace her gave her bragging rights, which she exercised frequently. She had continued to dye her hair blonde as she aged to hide the grey sneaking in, styled short and businesslike, she appeared still to be a career woman. But today she was wearing sandals and no stockings under her suit, so Anne and Marie had congratulated her on her informality. She was stocky of build, and dressed to make the most of the few curves she had left.

Over the small sandwiches, the delicate teacups, and luncheon plate covered with bite sized hors d'oeuvres, their conversation had gone from the ridiculous to the sublime. They were currently comparing oddities in their family histories, and so far, Frankie's family was out in front.

Her grandfather, Henri, from the 'Old Country,' had come to America in the 1850's and joined the Union Army during the Civil War, assigned to an infantry unit out of Pennsylvania. After the war, he married a young American and produced 6 or 8 children. His first wife died, and he fled the country, sans kids, leaving them to fend for themselves. And fend they did. The youngest son, Robert, settled in Michigan, started a lumber mill, built a small town around it and opened a power plant to supply the town. He became a leading citizen, wealthy and respected.

So upon hearing how well his son had done, indigent Henri skulked into town and tried to worm himself into Robert's good graces. As it happened, Robert was in a receptive mood, having just been told of his record-breaking fiscal year. Henri and Robert soon found they were of like souls; a deep and strong bond quickly grew between the men.

Henri settled into an upstairs bedroom of the family home and had all the tea and crumpets the housemaid could deliver. Having a roving eye and robust libido, Henri and the housemaid were soon 'in the family way,' and married quietly, though there was a 30 year difference in age. Again, the children came quickly, and soon three girls and three boys roamed Robert's mansion.   The fact was not lost upon Robert that these were actually his siblings, something which grated the man no end, though he kept quiet about it.

The father and son spent a lot of time together, much to the chagrin of the son's wife, Helen. What had begun as a small and happy adult family was now no less than chaos at its quietest moments. The children experienced little to no discipline, running and screaming through the mansion constantly. Hence Robert escaped by working in his beloved mill many hours of the day. When Henri was not beside his son at the mill, he holed himself and his young wife up in their room, inauspiciously attempting to create more and more babes.

One day as Henri reposed in his bedroom, there was an explosion at the mill, and a terrible fire destroyed the old structure. Dark heavy smoke filled the air of the town, making eyes water and faces black with soot for those who ventured outside. Word quickly reached Robert's home that he had been standing in the boiler room with several of the workers and there was little hope as to his survival.

Henri was devastated. The sun rose and set in his newfound relationship with his son. Henri became inconsolable, and soon left the country again to return to his homeland in Europe. Robert's widow paid the former housemaid (left with the 6 children) a handsome sum to extract herself and her offspring from the house, and went on to marry a doctor some years later. The housemaid took the money and the kids, went to her mother in Kentucky, and none were heard from again.

Henri, once more living by his libido, found a sweet young thing in France, married her (though still married to the housemaid), and began, once again, to leave proof of his manhood annually. This time there were only three when Henri passed away at 97. He died penniless, but the new wife, Mary, knew of the fortune Robert had made in Michigan. She and her three babies ventured across the Atlantic to claim her share. On the crossing, she discovered she was again with child.

Robert's widow, not being of strong constitution, considered the argument Mary brought that having the same father as Robert, her children were entitled to a portion of Robert's wealth. The poor widow could not stand up to the belligerence of Mary as well as the size of her belly, and signed over more than half of the remaining fortune, including title to the amazing mansion. This all on the condition that Mary leave the country in short order.

Mary, true to her word, left for Canada immediately with a carpetbag full of cash. But being a gambler, Mary went through the considerable inheritance in less than 3 years, so made her way to Florida where it was much less expensive to live. There she lived in a shanty, barely secure enough to keep the rain off her kids.

The youngest, James, or Jay as he preferred, left the family when he was 14, to go north and find his own fortune. He worked in Richmond for a while, getting a feel for being a young man of gentle upbringing, rather than the country bumpkin he felt like. Jay moved north to New York City, and was working as a runner on Wall Street on Black Friday when the stock market crashed. When he saw men hurtling themselves from windows, Jay fled the big city and landed in upstate New York. There he met the love of his life, married her, and brought her home to Florida to live. After WWII, a local high school was offering automatic high school diplomas to all veterans, but Jay did not qualify due to his birth outside the US.

But being very creative and ingenious, Jay falsified some records, had his mother swear he had been born in a tiny Florida town that had conveniently lost the town hall to fire, complete with the attending mid-wife's signed affidavit. Jay instantly became a US citizen, took his new papers to the high school, got his diploma, and then went to work on his education.

With papers stating he had been born in the US, many more doors were opened for him. He bought a small house, moved his mother into the back bedroom, and he, his wife, his young daughter, and his mother formed a closely knit family. We don't know what happened to the 'mid-wife.' But isn't it amazing that she was not only alive after all those years but also in the vicinity, readily available to sign some papers?

Jay went on to become a pillar of his community, teacher and counselor. He earned many degrees, including a doctorate in Elementary Education. Though the product of a promiscuous father without the benefit of legal marriage, Jay was now a bright spot in the family history.

Frankie took a sip of her cold tea from the delicate porcelain teacup; little finger extended upward in silliness, and dared one of the other two to match that tale. Frankie knew most of the tale was the truth, but felt her embellishments added to the story. Marie had listened with rapt attention, bending closer and closer to Frankie as the tale unwound, until her glasses, strung around her neck, had landed in her teacup. This caused another bout of frenzied laughter, and another look of stern disapproval from the waiter, who quickly reached to save the valuable little cup and saucer from further disrespect.

Anne had second thoughts about Frankie's story, but decided to leave it alone for the time being. She was full to nearly bursting with her tale of her dear Aunt Sally.

The three friends ordered dessert, giving the harried waiter hope that the rowdy trio was soon to vacate his quiet and orderly world. Alas, the poor man discovered all too quickly the error of his ways in serving them a dish, however small, of concentrated sugar.

The size of the portions of the sweet confections were again good reason to taunt the ill-fated waiter, the high-powered chef, and the little tea house in general.

The giggles soon subsided, and over fresh coffee, Anne began her tale.

"Now where is the best place to start?" Anne elaborately pondered while looking toward the tin ceiling, rubbing the second of her double chins.

"Why not the beginning? That seems pretty obvious!" Frankie was eager to give up the bandstand. She had been talking nearly non-stop since her story began, her two friends listening with rapt attention, their intent interest urging her on. Not that she needed much urging. Frankie could hold her own on any subject, anywhere, with anyone.

"I agree," noted Marie. "Start there."

"She is actually my cousin, but was called Aunt Sally when it made her seem older. She actually came from very humble beginnings, which are not really much to talk about. She was born and bred out west, mostly in northern California amongst the Sequoias and the redwoods. My mother used to tell me of how Aunt Sally would run and hide in the forest for days on end. Momma's sister would be beside herself with worry, on the verge of gathering the other townsfolk to form a search party, when Aunt Sally would appear suddenly. Invariably, she would head for the kitchen and dive into a loaf of fresh bread. Momma used to tell me it was as though Sally had a sixth sense for the bread. I guess the fragrance of the new bread threading through the big trees had nothing to do with it!"

This little joke sent the three of them into fits of laughter – again.

"Anyway," Anne continued, wiping a tear from her fat rosy cheek, "Much like your grandfather, Frankie, my Aunt Sally left home very young. There always were rumors of how her mother beat her, trying to mold her into a proper young lady, but nobody knows for sure. There was no father in the home – he left after the tenth or eleventh child. Sally's mother had to give up the last four or five after the father abandoned them, and the remaining family lived much on the kindness of others.

Sad situation for sure, but not too uncommon back then.

"Anyway, Sally went north. This in the mid to late nineteenth century and the Gold Rush in other parts of California was making history in a hurry. Sally wanted no part of it. She worked her way through Oregon, signing on as a cook in a logging camp. She was slight in build, so dressed as a boy and called herself Sal.

"She quickly decided this was way too much work; she was assigned the most appalling jobs in the cook tent. She peeled potatoes until her fingers turned pink, and washed pots nearly as tall as she. The hot water made her skin wrinkle and her fingernails soft. Even though she was playing the masculine role, deep down she kept the heart of a woman." Anne's hand went to her ample bosom and patted up and down as indication of a heart beating as she looked toward the heavens.

More giggles wafted through the air, much to the chagrin of the poor waiter. Most of the luncheon crowd had finished their meals and vacated the premises; he could only wish this Terrible Trio, as he now thought of them, would soon follow.

After a sip of now cold tea from the tiny cup, Anne continued, "Anyway, Sally worked as hard as she could, and still survived a bit of ribbing from the humongous man who was the main cook. She guessed from his actions that he had adopted her/him and served as protector. Sally was not of a mind to ignore this protection, so pushed it to the limit. She wandered the camp very late at night when all the loggers were passed out from either hard work or hard drink.

"She found some interesting things, among which was a small canvas bag of nuggets. Sally knew of the rush for gold to her south, and understood its worth, so into her pocket went the little bag."

"What a thief!" chimed Frankie and Marie nearly in unison.

"That's not all!" Anne's chubby finger waved back and forth as she continued, "Anything of value or potential value went by way of her secret stash: lockets, pocket watches, wool socks. She even stole a Bible!"

"Now that's low." Marie stated.

"It sure is. You can get one at any hotel!!" Frankie noted. And laughter exploded again.

With her ongoing story in tact, Anne said, "Well, it wasn't long before the loggers began to compare notes of items missing from their personal belongings, and concluded Sal in the kitchen was to blame since nothing had gone missing before he came to the camp. Several of the men went to Sal's tent to confront him, and found 'him' under the shower, all 'his' feminine jewels exposed. The men were shocked, and quickly backed away. All but one, and the story goes that he grabbed her and had his way with her right there and then. He used her several times during the next few days, keeping her in his tent tied to the cot in his absence, telling others the young girl had fled."

"How utterly awful! What was she then, fifteen or sixteen? Poor girl." Marie shook her blonde head, making tsk-tsk sounds with her tongue.

"Yes, it must have been awful for her, because the story goes that she escaped in the dead of night with her satchel of goods and the logger's boots. The camp searched for her the next day, but her years in the redwood forest near home made her invisible to the loggers, while she could watch them carefully.

"She stayed undercover in the depths of the forest for a while, nursing her wounds, both physical and mental. Sal became Sally again, though kept the overalls to protect her thin legs from scratches and insect bites as she traveled through the woods."

"You know, we don't have any idea what life was like 150 years ago" mused Marie.

Frankie nodded her agreement as Anne went on with her saga. "No, we don't. All we can surmise is that being sixteen then was a far cry from being sixteen now." All three heads bobbed in unison. "And the maintaining of one's virginity was tanta-mount to a good marriage, and now Sally had lost that to an evil and disgusting logger.

"Spring was quickly approaching, and Sally wandered in a northerly direction. She stopped in the smaller towns to trade her 'booty' for food and other needs. She soon found she was in a family way, adding to her distress. This meant going home to California and her family was now completely out of the question."

"The poor girl." Marie whined, her face distorted with the look of genuine pity.

"Poor girl, my ass!" blubbered Frankie. "You play, you pay! This is just her come-uppance for not getting away from that logger sooner!"

"But she was tied to the cot during the day," overprotective Marie countered with a logical reason for Sally's length of stay.

"You don't think Sally could have sneaked out any night she wanted to?" Frankie was indignant that Marie was so naive. "I think she enjoyed the sex once the initial hurt and embarrassment subsided. Who knows, she may even have decided to entertain more than the one logger."

Anne intervened with "We'll never know, and that point has been debated through the generations. Anyway, during a freak spring snow, as luck would have it, Sally stumbled onto the steps of a little chapel in Washington, near the Canadian border. The pastor was standing in the window watching the snow float down from the heavens – or so the story goes – and thought Sally had collapsed onto the steps when all she did was trip.

"Being a good and proper Christian, the pastor brought her inside where she stayed until the baby was born. Word has it that he even offered to marry Sally and raise the baby as his.

"Sally would, of course, have no part of that, and eventually vanished into the night, leaving the baby for the pastor to worry about."

Marie, the more stoic of the two listeners, was just mortified. "I'm just mortified! How can a mother leave her child after carrying him in the womb for so long?" Frankie, being the more pragmatic, simply wanted to know if it was a boy or a girl.

"It was a little girl, and we understand the pastor kept her and raised her. He named her after her mother, Sally, and gave her his own mother's middle name, Lynn."

"Sally Lynn. That's a pretty name," Frankie said, and Marie added, "Very lyrical, like Poe's Annabell Lee."

Anne was getting wound up and the telling of the story was becoming not only more animated, but also louder. The waiter had long ago cleared the table of all but the water glasses, which he kept filled. He never seemed to be very far from the table.

"Once Sally had successfully migrated from Washington into Canada, she pulled out the overalls, pulled back her hair and hid it under a hat, resuming her identity as Sal. As a member of the pastor's family, she had been privy to a lot of gossip and tall tale telling carried by the congregation members. Sally had learned of the discovery of gold in Alaska, on the Kenai Peninsula. She bought her way into a northern bound wagon train with most of her remaining trinkets stolen from the logging camp last year.

"It was an arduous trip, and even though it was summer, a lot of the frail died, mostly the women and children. Sally's shape had changed with the bearing of a child, becoming rounder and shapelier, more woman-like. She was having an increasingly more difficult time maintaining the visage of Sal."

"You know," Frankie interjected, "My late husband and I took sort of a wagon train trip from Seattle to Anchorage in our RV once. It was on a paved road, all the modern conveniences, and still very difficult. I can just picture some of the problems those people encountered."

Marie nodded in agreement and said, "All for the sake of gold."

This brought an unusual moment of quiet to the three friends before Marie and Frankie looked toward Anne to go on with the biography of her adventurous Aunt Sally.

"Well, if I remember the story, this trip through the Yukon Territory is where the tide turned for Sally. She had hitched a ride with a middle-aged couple, and two months into the trip, the Mrs. contracted a fever and died. Sally figured since everyone thought she was a boy, she'd just stay put. But the husband came to her bed one night and told her he knew she was a woman as he had seen her bathing in a creek. The choice he gave her was simple: service my needs or get out of my wagon. He even offered to pay her in the gold he had brought with him to stake his claim on a piece of this wilderness."

"Oh, my!" The phrase burst quickly from Marie's mouth.

"Well, what did you expect? Men are men, and 150 years hasn't changed much! They just do it now in cars and trucks instead of covered wagons." Countered Frankie.

"Be that as it may, Sally decided she had nothing to lose, literally, and service the man she did. At his request she maintained the appearance of Sal. The man told her it was to protect her from the others, but Sally figured it was to keep her for himself.

"A long summer later, the beat-up remains of the wagon train were in Alaska. Sally wasted no time in vacating her current position. She took all the hard-tack and jerky she could carry, along with the map of the area, and trudged through the forests."

"Like Brer Rabbit and the briar patch," muttered Frankie under her breath. This comment raised another chuckle from the three, and even brought a crooked smile from the hard-hearted waiter. He had ceased to lurk around the table and was standing unabashed nearby, leaning against the door jamb to hear the rest of the story.

"Yes, she was at home in the forest, that's for sure. Sally eventually wound her way to a small boom town, resplendent with the brown canvas tents and muddy streets. But it was civilization, of sorts, so she sat back and watched the town for a bit.

"It became obvious there were no women in the town, or very few as Sally could see none walking about. Needing money and a warm place to stay, she decided she had the best tool for money-making between her legs."

Marie's sharp intake of breath exploded in the silence of the now empty café.

"I know what you're thinking, Marie. But what choice did the poor girl have? She only did the best she could with what she had." Ever-logical Frankie defended Sally's decision.

The tiny chair squeaked in agony as Anne shifted her bulk before continuing. "Legend has it that she marched into the town, stood in the center of the tent city and announced her intentions. She was quickly met with a hoard of men of all shapes and sizes, who in the middle of the street tried to outbid each other for the right of being first."

Anne was in her glory. She was an animated storyteller and could see that her two companions were enthralled with the tale she was spinning. The tea in the delicate cups had long since grown cold, and the tiny sandwiches had been reduced to crumbs on their dainty doilies.

"Well, I never.....: Marie sputtered. "I just never!"

"And what did you expect she'd do?" Frankie rushed to Aunt Sally's defense. "She's in basically a foreign land, alone, and her precious virginity taken years ago. I have to give her credit for having the moxie to get money for what the men would eventually have taken anyway!"

Anne concurred. "From what I understand from all the family folklore, Sally was a real adventurer, sharp as a tack, and real-istic about her situation. She supposedly kept her wits about her during this frenzied bidding war, and ended up with not only a lot of gold, but also a good tent, several blankets to keep her warm, and a sturdy cot to keep her off the cold dirt floor. Well, her and any companions, anyway.

"She had quickly discovered the most powerful and respected man among the throng surrounding her, and wisely stopped the bidding when his was the highest, giving him the prized first place. After locating the tent she had won and moving her cot and blankets there, she invited the winner to capture his prize. Needless to say, it didn't take too long. Years of abstinence and all that, you know. "

Frankie sat back and howled at that, the waiter snickered audibly, and Marie turned beet red. At this pause in the story, the waiter bent to retrieve the little cups and plates, asking if the ladies would like more of anything. They responded in the negative, and the waiter said, "This is the end of my shift. I have enjoyed serving you today, Ladies."

Almost in unison, the three asked him to join them, which he politely refused. "But you will have to come in another day and let me know what happened to your Dear Aunt Sally. She sounds quite the character. Good bye."

The three women bid the man adieu, and Anne continued with her tale. "Where was I? Or rather where was Sally?"

"Earning her wage!" Marie burst forth with her face forming a forbidding frown. Anne and Frankie exchanged glances before Frankie's eyes went skyward and Anne took a breath to go on.

"Well, as you might guess, the first few days were difficult for Sally, being the only woman the men had seen in several years. For her own well being, Sally had to limit her visitors' time and limit the number of men each day. She also insisted her callers bathe before they entered her tent.

"Sally wasn't short on food, either. A few of the men actually had some manners left and invited her to join their campfire for a bowl of hot beans and cup of harsh coffee.

"After the first couple of months passed, the little town of tents settled into a peaceful routine, and Sally began to make more and more demands on her customers. They were all just so pleased with a young nubile woman in their midst, they barely noticed she had the only milk cow left in the area and a fine mule. She had all the gold she could ever use, so bartered her fancy for other functional items.

"We heard she stayed there for about five years, gathering whatever she thought she might need when she decided to return to California. She had amassed a large fortune, the cow, several good pack mules and was working" Anne made a motion of quotes with her hands "off a debt to take possession of a fine covered wagon."

"Well, it sounds like she had her ducks in a row, for sure." This from Frankie.

"I couldn't have ducks in that way." Marie shook her head slowly and muttered to her bosom. "I just can't imagine!"

With a flip of her hand Frankie told her friend, "You would never have left California to begin with, so all of the rest of the story is a mute point for you."

"That's probably true," Marie had to agree.

Frankie then quickly looked to Anne to continue her story before Marie got into more discussion about her own self.

"In the spring of the fifth year Sally was in Alaska, she heard of several men who had given up their claims and wanted to return to their families in the US. She sought them out and arranged for passage with them.

"After an arduous 5 month journey, she found herself in the small town of Vancouver, British Columbia, Canada, just north of the busy port of Puget Sound.
"Though Vancouver was nearly 100 years old by then, it was an unincorporated sawmill town and still rough around the edges. Nonetheless, compared to the tents in which Sally had lived, and flourished I might add, for the past few years, she recognized a wealth of opportunity lay at her feet.

"Her story goes that she checked into the hotel as Mr. Jones, stayed a few days, then evaporated into the night. Actually, she was going for dress fittings and supplying herself with all the feminine wiles available. Sally threatened the seamstresses with loss of life and limb if they ever mumbled a word of the transformation. After donning the new clothes, she rechecked into the hotel as Miss Sally Strawbridge Ledyard, lately of a small town near Philadelphia in the East.

"She told everyone that she had been traveling with her father, George Ledyard, who had some holdings nearby, but he had tragically become afflicted with the consumption, and she had to bury him in the Idaho territory. Boo hoo, boo hoo." Anne grinned at the wide eyes of her friends, especially Marie. Marie had led a sheltered life and this kind of adventurous woman was an enigma to her naive mind.

"How could she have changed so that no one recognized her?" Marie was genuinely perplexed. "There must have been some similar characteristics that people noticed in both... both.... people?"

Frankie jumped in to answer. "Now just think about it, Marie, if you saw a small man, covered with dust from travel, boots scuffed and coveralls filthy from wear, not to mention the smell after so long without a bath, then a week later you saw a delicately petite young woman with hair carefully piled under a stylish bonnet and matching gown, would you connect the two?"

Marie had to admit, even in a modern setting, a connection would be a slim chance. "But still, Anne, how did your cousin explain all her gold? All her money?"

"She simply told everyone it was her late father's, and it was her intention to follow his wishes and invest in the lumber industry there-about. This is where her time in that logging camp came in really handy. By being able to talk the talk, she managed to wangle a few really good deals in the industry. She ended up owning a sawmill of her own, which flourished under her tutelage. Along with 'other things'," Anne winked at Marie, who blushed slightly. "Sally had developed a keen business sense."

"She continued to run the mill, gathering wealth, for a couple of years. She wasn't in Vancouver very long at all. She sold the mill and the land she had purchased at a huge profit, and headed south. This time she traveled as Miss Sally Strawbridge Ledyard, grand dame of Vancouver. Her reputation preceded her to some extent as loggers were a mobile group and she was greeted everywhere like visiting royalty."

"Well, she ended up in San Francisco. By the time she arrived in that town, she had polished her manners, as it were, and carried herself with an air of authority that commanded respect before she said even one word."

"Now I'm wondering something," Frankie's furrowed brow indicated deep thought.

"OK, What?" Asked Anne as she thought she had been pretty detailed about her aunt, to the point of making stuff up to keep the story going.

"How old was Sally when she got to San Francisco? She must have been in her 30's, which was really old back then. Especially for a single woman. She would have been considered a spinster for sure."

"I think she was only in her mid 20's. Remember she ran away from home to the lumber camp in her early teens."

"That's still old for a single woman at that time in history. Didn't that hurt her overall?" It seemed as though Frankie was trying to trap Anne into some part of the story that didn't match.

"I'm not sure if it hurt her. All I know is that when she settled in San Francisco, she opened a bank account with all her accumulated fortune, and the banker loved her! But money didn't buy her everything, and the snobs on Nob Hill never let her crack into their circle.

"She eventually quit trying, bought a large house near the waterfront, recruited some beautiful women, and started a brothel. If she knew anything, she new how to sell ....."

"OK. OK. We understand what she sold! Didn't she ever do anything on the up and up?" Marie was concerned.

"I don't think so after she left Vancouver. But she was a huge success as she had the cleanest house, the prettiest women, thereby allowing her to charge the clients more than anyone else. Plus, she treated the men who frequented her establishment as though they were frequenting the bank, or the livery. She became very popular,"

"I'm sure!" interrupted Marie. "Didn't she ever marry or anything?"

"No, I don't think she did. But she did make sure her daughter, Sally Lynn, was well off. Sally sent large and anonymous donations to the pastor in Washington with instructions at least half be used to care for and educate Sally Lynn. Her will also left all her money and land to her daughter, and a personal letter to be delivered only upon her death."

Frankie wanted to know: "OK, so how long did she have this House of Ill Repute and what eventually happened to her?"

"She died in the big earthquake of 1906. Now I don't know if it's true, but family legend has it that when the earthquake hit, the epicenter was right under her business, and the mansion and all its inhabitants and glamorous settings were completely swallowed up and never heard from again."

Frankie smiled and Marie shook her head slightly as she spoke, "Fitting end, for sure, straight to Hell by the direct route! You couldn't get more melodramatic! I'm not sure I believe you. Do you know what happened to the daughter? To Sally Lynn?"

"Yeah. I'd like to know that, too! What did happen to Sally Lynn?" Even skeptical Frankie's curiosity spewed forth.

Anne sat back on the little chair, assumed a smug face and said, "She's my mother!"

End

The

Bog

Author's Note:

The inspiration for this tale came in the early 1990s in Northern Virginia as I drove to and from work.

My husband really liked the story, but I thought it was awful. So I 'lost' it.

He found a copy in 2006 he had kept in an old stack of papers, and asked me to finish it.

So it is now a work in progress. It has changed substantially from the prose written here. The newer story will appear in a future volume.

I hope you enjoy this early version.

The Bog

Sometimes, when conditions are right – just exactly right – with the sun and the wind and the rain, a little bog of green comes suddenly to life in the Deep South. In the shadows of the foot-hills slightly east of the Shenandoah Valley, not far from the Great Falls in the Potomac River, this gentle awakening usually comes near the end of winter when the heavy grey clouds are still lurking in the skies above the distant mountains and the sweet jonquils are peeking through the last vestiges of snow.

The barren brown of the winter on the very threshold of explod-ing into blossom brings this one little wash between the rocks and the trees to life and begins teeming with lives of sparse and long-lived acquaintances. If one were to find this area, this once drab and winter-dead acre, one would scarcely make note of it other than to possibly wonder why it is so different, why it came to be so green first, while all the surrounding trees and vines are still cast in their dowdy winter's garb. Very few peo-ple take the bother, take the time to wander through the moldy leaves and fallen vines and decayed trees to make the trek to the patch of green in this mildly wooded terrain. But if they should, if ever they would, what magic they would see.

Among the green foliage lives a band of Folk, not dissimilar to the Gypsies and Wanderers of old. They laugh, they love, they play, they hunt and reap harvests, just as any other set of people in the world. Their world, however, *** is contained *** consists solely in this green bog which blossoms only when conditions are right – just exactly right.

These people know not that they are different, or that their lives are interrupted intermittently by conditions which are not just exactly right. They only sense that they must deeply live every single moment, and do so with an abandonment in play and unexplained sense of importance in each task.

They reap their tiny harvests, they dance their ancient folk-dances; the Ladyfolk sew their stylish costumes with little needles wrought of very tiny pieces of metal. The metal from which the Menfolk fashion the needles, as well as eating utensils and other things needed is taken from extraordinarily large cylindrical containers found in the nearby fields. The objects are completely enclosed except for a pear shaped opening on one of the flat ends large enough for a grown Manfolk to climb through standing nearly upright.

Inside the cylinders is dark and some have a heady sweet fragrance or the stench of the forest floor after a long dismal rain. The metal of these objects is softer than the metal in the things the Folk find in the ground covered with rust. So needles are made from the material gathered from the cylinders, as well as bowls for the tables and pots for the fires. The heavier metals are brought to the fires, the rust scraped completely off, and oil rubbed carefully on each surface.

The little company of folk appears only for a day and a night in regular time, but to them it is like the passing of the sun: like a year to normal time. The night is their winter, their Darkseason in which nothing grows, most animals sleep, and it is cold and miserable and hard to do productive work outside. It is the time reserved for the building of things inside, the fixing of small things broken, and the mending of tools and furniture. The Menfolk work with the large tools they have forged during the Lightseason from the harder heavier metals protected by the oil.

The Ladyfolk use Darkseason to spin fine threads from the dried foliage and make clothing, curtains, cloths for the tables and chairs, and to make babies.

The Ladyfolk gather together and use their tiny fingers to make ever so tinier stitches which grow into coats for their Menfolk, dresses and aprons for themselves and buntings for the babies. The Ladyfolk also use Darkseason to cook long and hot dinners, since the heat from the fires warms the little shelters in which these tiny people abide.

The fires are kept aglow at all times, and in the coldest hours, are stoked to the very limits of the ovens. The Menfolk manipulate pieces of hot hard metals into heavier hand tools to till the soft and aromatic soils of Lightseason.

It seems that each and every bog-year turns slowly into Lightseason just in time, just as all the supplies hoarded are becoming dangerously low. As youngsters the world over ponder "How high is up?" some of the Childfolk wonder at how the lessening of the supplies brings on the Lightseason and wonder if they secreted some of the supplies away, how much sooner the boring Darkseason would go away. The wee ones enjoyed the idea they may have some control over the light and dark.

In the first fragments of Lightseason, the Menfolk are donning the coats and tee-tiny hats that have been made over the Darkseason by the Ladyfolk. They are taking up the new and shiny tools they have made during the long and cold time of Darkseason. It is time to begin to venture away from the warm and cozy shelters to begin the rituals of gardening for their fresh food and the foods that will be saved for next Darkseason.

In the very first misty rays of Lightseason, they clear away the frosty debris which has fallen on their garden patches, gently nurturing the bulbs and tubers into life. As the shadows of

Darkseason diminish, the rays of light help to dispel some of the bone-chilling cold felt by the Menfolk.

The Menfolk laugh hard as they work harder and make good friendships as they team together, bringing their charge to a peak harvest for all to enjoy.

It was during an early time of the Lightseason when Jado, a big strapping person bounding with muscles and good humor, came upon a crack in the earth climbing up a dirt wall which was the westernmost limit of their area. He did not recall it from past Seasons, so called his friends over to take a look. They all peered into the darkness of the deep crevasse, which actually seemed to grow as they watched. They were all apprehensive of the new discovery, and leery of venturing too very close.

Some of the older men began to tease Jado, shouting it was his cave since he was the one who had happened upon it; they were using the "Finders-keepers" logic with which they had been raised since childhood.

Jado was not amused, but neither was he about to show the whole of the village, elders and youngers, that he held fear of anything in his heart. He wanted to appear cautious, careful and courageous, especially in the beautiful eyes of his ladylove, Marlina. So he approached the growing fissure with stealth, and bent forward slowly so as to see inside.

It was dark. It was very very dark and Jado could see nothing. He motioned to the mumbling company of Menfolk behind him to quiet, and pointed his ear toward the hole to listen. He could hear only the soft rustle of the early leaves of Lightseason. He turned his nose toward the place and sniffed mightily, but could smell only the sweet fragrance of new buds of flowers and trees.

He was at a loss. To move forward, closer to the widening gap required much more courage than poor Jado possessed. To move back, however, would make him look weak in the eyes of his peers. And his beloved Marlina. Jado felt a trickle of perspiration roll down his thick neck and decided to take the middle ground.

"This is a strange thing." Jado's booming voice reverberated across the frosty acreage. "We must approach it with care. We must protect the Childrenfolk and Ladyfolk from its possible danger. I will stand guard here while you find rope to tie around the trees." Jado indicated the selected trees with a broad sweep of his huge and muscular arm.

No one moved. All the Menfolk stood stock still and stared at Jado. They seemed reluctant to go for fear of missing something.

"Go!!" Jado bellowed in his most authoritative baritone voice. "Go quickly and find rope!"

The men were on the move before the echo of Jado's words returned to the bog. They turned and walked toward the center fire in the village. A few of them mumbled beneath their breaths at Jado's bravado, but still wandered in the general direction of the ropes Jado had requested.

Jado breathed a silent sigh of relief, and turned back toward the opening. He jumped back quickly as he caught sight of the new outlines of the chasm. It had grown along the ground to nearly touch his foot. Nervous perspiration gathered on his brown brow, and his heart beat quickly. This thing at his feet was a black hole the likes of which had not been encountered by himself or anyone else. The depth of this unknown made Jado shiver at the possibility that some thing grave and awesome could befall his peaceful village.

Nowhere in the history volumes he had read or tales of the elders he had heard anything parallel to this mystery. He knew that this point in time could be very dangerous because the little Childfolk would be so active with their energies, running and jumping and giggling as they do. Jado was afraid the Childfolk would let their curiosity get the better of them and fall into the crevice. It was already large enough to swallow a full grown Manfolk, and was still parting! The fissure was frightening – still very black, very dark, and very very scary.

Some of the Menfolk were now returning with rope and sticks to offer some meager protection of the gap. They quickly tied a barrier around trees far from the grotto, guessing, or rather hoping, the area they encompassed would be large enough in the end.

The Menfolk decided, too, that someone would stay by the crack in the land and announce changes as they occurred, then bent their imaginations as to what was happening to their precious space.

Boleko was the first to take the watch. He volunteered for the duty because he knew this would probably be the safest time, especially if the hole kept growing. So far it was only great danger to the Childfolk, and the temporary fence of rope would delay their encroachment.

Some of the Childfolk called him Boleko the Bully. He was very large, very loud, and many of the Childfolk had seen Boleko cringe at the sound of his mother's voice. They had seen him jump at the snap of a twig and had known him to be a coward and run from fights. The Childfolk set traps for him and laughed at him. It was unusual for him to come forward to do this task, and the Childfolk wondered if Boleko knew something special about this New Water.

Boleko was surprised when a small spout of steam spewed from the fissure. The burst of steam came suddenly, and blew little droplets of warm water all over him. Considering the chill of the air, the warmth felt good. But it may have been ice water for all the comfort it brought to Boleko who ran away quickly toward the area where the other Menfolk were again working on the gardens.

"The hole is spewing hot water! It is spitting out hot water!" He called as he ran. "Come quick!! Come and see the steam!" Boleko nearly tripped over his own large boots as he motioned frantically toward the liquid squirting from the earth with his large hands and arms.

The Menfolk looked quickly amongst themselves, and in unison dropped their tools and ran pell-mell over the rocky and barren land to the fissure, which was spewing nearly a fountain into the air by this time. Boleko followed closely behind the last Manfolk.

The water was warm still, and had an unusual odor. The

aroma was unfamiliar, but not displeasing in the air. As the droplets fell upon the Menfolk, they rubbed their fingers and hands together, noticing the slippery feel of the emulsion.

"I wonder what it is," said one of the Menfolk.

"Maybe the land is going to explode!" cried another.

Jado said, "I don't think so. Look how it makes a fountain and no longer grows higher. The hole is no longer growing, either. It is the same as when we left before. There is still a lengthy distance from the ropes."

The others looked around them, and satisfied themselves that Jado was correct. With the acceptance of this thought, their bodies lost the attitudes of silent fear. Then they became curious.

"Oh. Look at the ground!" Boleko yelled. "It becomes soft where the water touches." Boleko's boot sank into the earth easily as he pushed with his heel.

The ground had, indeed, become soft and malleable where the droplets of the fountain's strange liquid and steam had landed. It appeared the fissure in the ground was giving them a gift. The soil was not so hard to work with their tools around the new water.

One of the Elderfolk standing outside the rope suggested, "We should cover our garden area with this liquid. And we should hurry before the elixir evaporates. If it will make our work easier in our fields, then it is a gift we should not ignore."

The Menfolk did consider this fearsome find to be good fortune, and quickly garnered buckets from the Ladyfolk to collect the solution. They carried the buckets to their garden spots and scattered the elixir over the ground with little cups. They took great care to be meager with the spreading of the stuff; the Menfolk wanted to be sure to have enough to cover the entire gardening area. They could make the trip more times if necessary. The fountain could be taken away as quickly and suddenly as it had been given.

Wondering if the water were potable, the Elderfolk standing by the phenomenon cupped his old and wrinkled hand to hold some of the liquid. The fluid dripped through his fingers with knuckles swollen with the maladies of age, but he retained enough in his palm with which to experiment. He held it to his nose, and finding no obnoxious odor, gingerly tasted it. It seemed sweet. It seemed innocent. "I have seen many long and fruitful Lightseasons, if this is to be my last," the Elderfolk thought, "Then I shall go by helping my Folk with this New Water ."

Unbeknownst to the others, the Elder put his hand to his mouth and drank all the liquid. Because of the consistency of the stuff, it slid easily down his throat. As it passed into his old stomach, the Elder felt a warmth, a pleasant warmth, permeate his body. He waited to see what would happen to him, standing very close to a large tree in case he felt the need to lean upon something. Minutes passed, the warmth inside subsided and no ill effects befell the Elder. He captured another handful, larger this time, and immediately drank it all down. He felt nothing but the warm sensation. The Elder wandered over to the Ladyfolk area, grabbed a cup and unobtrusively made his way back to the fountain.

The Elder filled the cup, drew it to his crinkled face, touched it to his lips and drank it all full down. At this point the Elder, though he felt no ill effects, sat at the root of the tree, adjusted his hat over his eyes, and feigned sleep so he could analyze his condition over a period of time.

Many of the Menfolk secretly hoped this incident would become a permanent water source for the village. The river to the south which normally supplied their water could be angry. It had taken many lives in the past. This, if it remained as it had for a while, was closer, and appeared much safer if the Ladyfolk and Childfolk stayed away from the edge. Jado was already planning a fence to build with a door heavy enough to keep the Childfolk out, but still manageable for the Ladyfolk. The fence would be a good project for the Menfolk in this Lightseason.

Hope was high in the air as the new liquid was sprinkled carefully over the old garden. The day had begun with some fearsome happenings, but seemingly had changed to good fortune.

The Childfolk, meanwhile, were alive with being able to finally run from the shelters, yelling their pleas until the mothers bundled them in all the clothes they could stand up in. They now could hop and jump and out into the early Lightseason they romped.

The Boyfolk are looking for the creatures that are crawling in and out of the ground and rocks, the creepy crawly things waking from Darkseason's hibernation. The little Boyfolk would try to trap the lizards, but their thickly gloved hands had little control over the petite reptiles. If a gloved hand did manage to hold its prey, the lizard would simply shed its tail and run under a rock, much to the chagrin of the little Boyfolk. The tikes chased after the crawly things as the critters all ran away in terror of the bundles of moving arms and legs which shriek suddenly and fall down frequently. The ladybugs would simply fly out of harm's way

The Girlfolk, on the other hand, were holding hands in a wee circle, dancing around and singing as loud as they could. They tripped on the uneven ground and fell to the cold earth in a fit of giggles. The holding of hands would drag several of the small damsels to the ground, and they would all lie in the warmth of the early Lightseason sun and laugh very hard.

It was a happy and peaceful, however noisy, scene to behold. The Menfolk were tending to the gardening, made easier with the delightful new liquid. The Boyfolk were chasing the bothersome critters out of the area. The Girlfolk were busily giggling and struggling to arise from the ground in all their layers of clothing. The Womenfolk were busy cleaning the floor coverings and taking large pieces of furnishings out into the fresh air after a long Darkseason closed up inside.

It is all the Menfolk can do to keep the garden places safe from little feet chasing many-legged pets across the even rows of tender and quickly growing seedlings. The new opening in the earth near the village brought special danger. The Menfolk feared for the lives of their little ones, and decided the man-hours lost from daily chores to watch over them were well spent to protect their charges.

Early in Lightseason, the river to the south is red and opaque. It is soon swelling to its bank's edges, constantly rising, slowly creeping every higher. Even though the very life of the clan depends on this body of water, it can be a very dangerous thing.

Frequently, the Ladyfolk bring their little buckets to catch some of the calmer water, pooling near some stones and roots, for their chores of cleaning and washing things. Never do the Ladyfolk venture to the riverside alone, for once, long long ago, a special person was taken by the river. She was Marlina, Jado's betrothed.

Pretty Maidenfolk Marlina took her buckets for her chores alone because all the other Ladyfolk were busy, and she didn't want to interrupt them.

She never returned. One of her buckets was found far down-stream, caught on the side of the river in the fork of a branch.

All the folks of the village fondly recall the lovely Marlina. She lent a smile to all who knew her, and had a happy word to say to all. Jado and Marlina had been a pair for many years, beginning as Childfolk. It was expected that they would join soon and start a family. She had but reached her marrying age when the tragedy struck.

This was a very sad time for everyone, especially Jado. At the sudden and awful loss of his Ladylove, Jado sank into the depths of despair until he could barely function. His excitement of this new discovery was more animation from him that the village had seen since the tragedy.

Marlina went one day about her normal chores and was no longer among them the next. The other Ladyfolk recalled the last time they had seen her. She went about her work of bringing water to her homestead, caring nothing for the troubles of the world. A song was on her lips when she began the chore.

As she picked up the two buckets, fastened them to the little hooks of wood, she brought the curved branch to rest across her shoulders. Marlina strolled with the empty buckets swinging jauntily in unison with the ruffles of her skirts. She thought about the pleasant evening she had spent with her family the day before. She smiled inwardly thinking of the teasing her father had given about her friendship with Jado, and her eyes sparkled with residual laughter. She walked down the path to the swollen creek, and heard a voice behind her call out: "Watch your step, Marlina, the river is angry today. Best to care it doesn't take you in."

She turned, making the empty buckets bob and sway as she nodded and yelled, "Thank you. I will be careful."

As she looked ahead to the winding path, she noted rocks and stubs of grass which could trip her on her return. When she came closer to the water, she could hear the soft roar of the running stream, usually quiet and no more than a trickle of gentle waves. She mentally repeated the warning to herself, and stepped lightly on the bank. She laid the branch on the ground and disconnected the empty buckets.

On the bank of the stream, there was a fallen tree which hung over the waters and formed a small inlet of sorts which usually held still water. This was the place where Marlina liked to draw clear water for cooking. The tree and its roots afforded her a good foothold and the stillness of the water in that protected place usually meant crystal clear liquid which needed little or no settling time before use.

Today was different, though. The storms in the mountains had caused much more rain than usual, and the quiet little inlet was overrun by the rushing waters crowding the banks and bushes growing nearby. The fallen tree where Marlina usually perched to draw up her buckets was all but covered with the swirling mud and the still water she sought had disappeared in the swollen brook.

Marlina wondered if the fissure and the liquid from Jado's discovery earlier had enhanced the fury of the little stream. The land had moved and the course of the water in the stream had been forced to a new path.

The young Maidenfolk looked carefully up and down the riverbanks for a safe place from which to pull her water. She wanted a place to yield her some clear water, not full of mud and mulch. Finding none, she decided that her fallen tree perch would be the best after all, feeling a point of familiarity with it.

Marlina perched on the base of the tree trunk at it's thickest part. Ordinarily she made her way more toward the end of the branches where the water was a little deeper so she could fill the buckets with one dip, but the swollen creek had already covered her tree trunk to that point.

Marlina fervently wished she had more water stored in her little kitchen. This strong, swirling, curling mass of quickly moving mud and branches gave her a fright, and she again instructed herself to take extra care against the angry torrent.

She pointed a slippered foot to a spot a bit in front of her, but as she bent her weight to it, she did not feel a secure footing. She pulled back and removed her slipper. Her second attempt felt a surer grip with her bare foot. She shook off her other shoe, and nestled both feet firmly at the base of the big tree trunk, lodging herself as steadfastly as she could and staying out of the quickly moving waters.

As Marlina reached back for the first bucket, a bit of the bark under her feet slid away, and she found herself with one foot in the water. Her skirts were dangerously close to the mud and muck. She quickly scrambled back to the top of the tree trunk and readjusted her position.

"I do wish I had done this before," Marlina thought to herself. "The water was so much calmer."

She knew the little stream had angered overnight and now seemed hungry for victims. Resolutely Marlina vowed she would not succumb to the lure of the waters.

Testing her footing again, she felt a good place, and carefully dipped the first bucket into the whirling muck under her feet. At the first touch of the current to the top of the bucket, the water lunged into the opening and nearly caught Marlina off balance. She grabbed for the shoreline and her hand brushed a knob of root of the fallen tree. The current was too strong.

The swift and swirling water tore the bucket from Marlina's hand, and she watch helplessly as it bobbed around the tree trunk and finally floated to the center of the torrent and was pulled quickly into the rushing, undulating, violently bubbling waters.

"Now I have to get another bucket!" Marlina admonished herself, "Either that or draw water every day. Well, I still have the one good bucket; I need to get back to do my other work."

Knowing the power of the waters, she now used a different method with her other bucket. She placed the bottom of the bucket in the water first and tipped the top away from the current. The water slowly arched around the opening, and though the container was difficult to control, Marlina was able to fill it.

Pleased that she didn't lose both buckets, she lifted this very full one out of the waters. Finding it quite heavy to manage with one hand, she released her hold on the root at the shoreline and brought her arm around to pull the bucket the final distance to the shore.

Just at that moment the tree trunk on which she was perched heaved, the dirt around the roots having been softened by the higher water, and she dropped her bucket. She lunged after it, grabbing for the handle before the creek claimed it for its own. Her skirts fell into the water and became heavy with the mud. The quagmire began to suck Marlina down, seeming to have evil fingers plucking at her skirts, pulling her slowly into their depths.

Marlina surrendered the bucket and tried to pull herself back to the top of the tree trunk. The extra weight of her small form and the pressure from the swirling mud tugging at her skirts were the undoing of the old dead tree. The massive joint of wood, branches and roots having pulled free of the shore, were at the mercy of the raging waters. The ***gnarled old wood was pulled into the mainstream of the flow.

Marlina screamed, but the water was too loud and hid the plea for help. The water was too strong and held tight to its prey. As she tried to swim to the shore, the roots of the tree she had depended upon for so many Lightseasons entangled her skirts and hugged her feet, pulling her under the waters as a friend would pull another along to an adventure. She tasted mud and saw a blackness. Her last thoughts were of her lost buckets.

After Marlina was lost, to protect the other precious young Ladyfolk from this danger, it was decreed that no fewer than two may take buckets to the river. The trail to the river was now called "Marlina's Trail." All who have gone with their buckets to the riverside since had returned safely.

This possible new source of water was an excitement for the Ladyfolk. If it were pure and clear, the danger of the stream would never be tested again. These days their gossip always included fervent wishes to be able to use the new discovery.

The Ladyfolk are hard put to keep the Childfolk from danger of the torrential waters. The sound of the water lapping over the stones and sticks is very inviting, and the sight of the waves fighting with the rocks and branches, curling around into inviting eddies and splashing freely in the rapids is nearly too much for the Childfolk to ignore. It seems, though, that the Childfolk have an innate respect for the river, and never dare to venture too close to the steep banks on their own. The frequently recall among themselves the lone bucket caught in the fork of a branch.

At mid Lightseason, when the garden is planted and the water less intense, the Menfolk will hide under the chore of watching the Childfolk by the river to sit in shady spots with little sticks and strings to catch the delicacies hiding the calmer clearer waters. Every now and again, a large wet and wiggly creature will come up on the end of a bit of string a Manfolk has dredged through the water. This is cause for a party and a celebration of the life they are granted is held at works end.

Every tiny pot and every tiny bowl is filled with the goodness of the bounty from the earth at that time. All the Childfolk of the community are sent searching through the field of tall grass for the blooms of Lightseason. They return with pockets bulging, little arms full and hearts truly light. All the fresh and fragrant flowers are brought to the center of their special table. This is the table which was wrought by all the hands of the citizenry to be used in important and happy celebrations. Celebrations such as this one.

The Darkseason fire is coaxed from the lazy coals, and in spite of the extraordinary heat, all the folk of the tiny band busy themselves to make a great feast of the slimy creature with its mouth at the very end of its long body and no legs or arms with which to walk or carry things. The creature is wrapped carefully and completely in squares of treasured thin and pliable metal which blow across the land. It is then placed upon the fiery coals to cook.

Two wide concentric circles are drawn the circumference of the fire pit, behind which must stand all the citizens of the town. The closer circle is the limit for the Childfolk and the outer band the circle for the Grownfolk. All the ears of all the neighbors are pointed toward the fire trying to be the first to hear the sizzle from the cooking. This is the person, Lady-, Child- or Manfolk who will be allowed to sit at the head of the table for the feast. When that sound is heard, all work stops, for by the time all the tools and implements are cleaned and in their proper places, the juices from the cooking will have been drained for a tasty gravy and the long and smooth life form will lie on the table for the feast. It is a happy time.

As Lightseason lengthens the humidity in the air and the harsh heat of the season press down on the little culture of people and makes them secretly wish again for Darkseason and the chill wind of the north.

But the bounty is heavy this time, and through the hot and humid air the Menfolk must reap the large harvest which has sprung from the sandy earth. The fruits and vegetables will be put carefully into tiny containers to carry their freshness throughout the next Darkseason.

The water from the skies had been sparse this Lightseason. and the Menfolk used little buckets to carry water to keep the gardens green and growing. All their bent backs and blistered hands have now created even more to do, but a gathering of foods such as this is much hoped for. Even the Ladyfolk lay down their cook spoons to help glean the fruits from the bushes and the vegetables from the earth.

Everyone laughs and makes great fun and sport of the harvesting, until the Childfolk feel they surely must be missing something, and soon come to lend their little fingers to the toil. Many of the berries plucked with little fingers found their way into little mouths, but many more went in the baskets.

The Menfolk wondered if the liquid from the new bubbling caldron discovered early in Lightseason enhanced the harvest. They vow to try to save some of the liquor from the clear pool over Darkseason in case the puddle does not return.

At last, all is finished. Darkseason grabs relentlessly at the eastern skies, and the chill in the air confirms that it is near. The last of the little containers is finally filled with the bounty of the harvest, and this Darkseason will not see empty shelves and dishes at its end. The Menfolk take their worn and weary shovels one last time to the earth, turning it under again and again, smoothing the roughness with little rakes, teeth broken from all the use in this fruitful Lightseason. Repairing these tools is one of the chores to be done by the fires of Darkseason.

The protective wrappings long since shed by the Childfolk in deference to the heat of mid Lightseason are dragged out and donned again, only to find sleeves too short and pants too tight.

Childfolk grow quickly in Lightseason. Some Childfolk have become Ladyfolk and Menfolk, and leave behind the chasing of bugs and crawly things. The Ladyfolk will sew with tiny needles the new capes and coats for growing Childfolk and patch elbows and knees for the things that still fit. The fires of this Darkseason will see busy fingers.

The fires of Darkseason will see also old Menfolk and old Lady-folk disappear into the darkness when their time is come to walk alone. The fires of Darkseason will see new babies created. All will grow in anticipation of the next Lightseason.

An interruption is coming across the mountains to the west. The conditions are shifting, and becoming not just exactly right. This is the time when the sun and the wind and the rain change, blowing a pause into the little bog. For a time it becomes one of the brown and dead winter acres; the little wash between the rocks and trees is quiet and empty and the new source of liquid is naught but a crack in the clay. All nestled quiet and still in the long shadows of the foothills of the Shenandoah Valley.

And so it shall remain until the next time conditions are right . . . .

Just exactly right.

The End